Rozalyn 3

Shan

Rozalyn 3

ISBN 978-0985711313

This is dedicated to my loves, Stevien, Zhaniah, & Zamaria
To everyone who has stood by my side and has supported me
from day 1. Love you! Muahh!

Acknowledgments

I would like to thank GOD for giving me the ability to be able to create stories that people have grown to love and look forward to. If it wasn't for him and the talent that he has blessed me with then none of this would be humanly possible. For that I am truly grateful.

To my children, I really am very proud of you guys because you have been truly patient and understanding of mama's writing. There were times when I've had to flat out ignore every last one of you, and not once did ya'll ever get mad and look at me differently. I thank ya'll for allowing me to work and for having a huge amount of patience. LOVE YA'LL WITH ALL OF MY HEART.

To my mother Lucy Miles, I really appreciate everything you've done for me. All the help and support you have given to me from keeping the kids when I needed to write, looking out for me when I was super tired from being up all night. Everything. You are more than a backbone for me and I appreciate it. Love you to pieces!

To my dad and step mother Robert and Linda Richardson, thank you so much for all for your continued support. Thank you for spreading the word about your daughter and looking out continuously for the kids and I. Love ya'll dearly.

My sister Sho! Thanks honey for all that you do. Love you! To my brother Julius I love you dearly!

My sister Ja'Lisa Taylor, thank you so much for your continued support for telling everyone who is anyone about my books. For showing me so much love, I love you! Thank you, thank you, thank you!

To my sister from another mother Jolita Coit, girl I love you dearly. I am so thankful to have met you in this life and truly appreciate everything that you have done for me. All of the support you given me, spreading the word, and helping me to sell these books. Thank you! Love you girl!

To my best friends Sharonda and Shay! Thank ya'll so much for everything you have done. Thank you for supporting me before I was even a published author. Thank you for spreading the word about me and just continuing to show love.

My auntie Tricia, thank you so much for the love and support.

Ellis Cottingham, thank you for continuing to show love and support and the wonderful word that you continue to spread. Thanks so much!

To Sonia Moore. Roni LaShae, Lola Monroe, Rosalyn Reed, Jennifer Lee, Wanda Lee Bawss, Jennifer Bawss Brooks, Charise Bee Heggs, Kenyetta Patrick, Danielle GhettoFabulous Gulley, Alex Brooks, Candice Williams, Laurie Robinson Thomas, Alicia Hartley, Angel Ramdorsingh, Marsha KT, Me'Tova Hollingsworth, Laquana Mccall, Natissha Wearethemajors Hayden, Jazz Bee, Saima Mann, Christine Fortes, Tiffany McGhee, Naeemah LadyBawss Sims-Leak, Keena Brown, Nicki Williams,Chris Johnson, Angel Ramdorsingh, Niecy Lansden-Martin, Raychelle ImJusChelle Williams, Hbic Ladyb Johnson, Nicole Coleman Primer, Kristie Fluker, Shannon Joshua, Verkisha D Searight Cook, Adrienne

Willis, Cassandra Mercer, Tyra Tee, Rebbeca N Ortiz, Kenyetta Patrick, Judy Thompson, Laurie Robinson Thomas, Shayla Che'Ri Perry, Candice Williams, Wendy Otey, Monica Fleming-Cadena, Bawss Mary Makesithappen Gordon, Debbie Gordon Harper, Tiesha Johnson, Christine Joyner I love every last one of you so much and I thank you all for everything that you have done to support me. I thank you for interacting with me, showing me mad love. I love you all! Muahh!

Special shout out to Gabrielle Dotson for everything that you do ma. I love you to pieces girl.

Special shout out to CoCo Bawss Mixon for always showing mad love, supporting me to the fullest, and spreading the word. #TBRS.

A very special shout out to Mo, Bigmofrombflo Boyd. You are truly heaven sent and I appreciate you so much for sticking by my side and supporting me to the fullest. I love you for that girl. Thanks for all you do. Muahh!!

Thank you to Tiesha Johnson for always throwing me those encouraging words, Winter Cromer, Kristine Beaman, Dama Cargle, Monique Chanae. Damn to just everybody that loves me you know exactly who you are. I'm going off the top of the dome right now so I know I have forgotten plenty of people but just know that it truly isn't intentional. Love ya'll with everything in me! Believe that!

To all the Facebook book clubs I thank you all for all the love and support you have thrown my way. I love each and every last one of you all: Team Bankroll Squad, The Takeover, Urban Book Lovers, Black Faithful Sisters and Brothers Book Club, My

Urban Books Club, We Read Urban Fiction, Diamond Eyes Bookclub, Black E-Book Club, A Day Early Publishing, Readers R Us, Just Read Book Club, Embellish, Fun(4)daMental, and so many more.

I would like to say a very special thank you to my new-found family, one that I am very happy to be a part of. If you didn't know Team Bankroll Squad is the squad! Shout out to my family David Weaver, Tremayne Johnson, Cole Hart, & Torica Tymes and the whole TBRS Family! Much Love to you all!

Thank you, thank you to David Weaver for all the advice that you have given me, for taking the time out to explain things to me when I didn't understand, and just passing along the wisdom. I truly appreciate it all, and respect that fact that you've done everything to help me in this game and not take advantage of me. I am truly honored to be a part of TBRS!

Table of Contents

Prologue: Tamar..1

1: Rozalyn..9

2:Rozalyn..25

3: Tamar..35

4: Rozalyn..43

5: Tamar..55

6: Rozalyn..67

7: Messiah..77

8: Tamar..87

9: Rozalyn..99

10: Tamar..109

11: Rozalyn..115

12: Messiah..119

13: Rozalyn..127

14: Messiah..141

15: Tamar..147

16: Rozalyn..153

17: Messiah..159

18: Brandon..165

19: Rozalyn..173

20: Tamar..179

21: Latoya...189

22: Rozalyn...193

23: Messiah..201

24: Rozalyn...207

25: Tamar..215

26: Messiah..221

27: Tamar..225

28: Rozalyn...233

29: Tamar..239

30: Messiah..247

31: Rozalyn...253

32: Tamar..257

Prologue: Tamar

Dear Tamar,

Wow it has been a long time since we have spoken and all I can do is say how bad I miss you. Even if the times we spent together were short lived they were the best times of my life. I find myself thinking of you every time I'm with my husband.

Often times when I'm having sex with him it's you that I am thinking of. I know that you told me to not contact you anymore because you were going to do right by your wife but I can't help myself. I'm in love with you Tae, and I don't mind playing the background to your wife as long as you continue to see me.

Baby I need you so bad. The way you touch me when we're together sends volts of electricity through my body; a feeling I've never felt before. Tae, I really need to see you and talk to you, please contact me with your new number. Don't leave me out here wanting you like this. I've tried my hardest to respect your wishes and not come by your house but it's been so hard for me.

If you truly, truly feel in your heart that you can do without me then I will accept that and try my best to move on. But before I do there is something that you must know. The day of your friends wake I was there Tae. I know that you asked me not to come around anymore but I just had to be there to see you and ensure that you were doing okay. After hearing you speak about your friend and seeing the love you were showing to your wife I became so emotional. I ended up in the ladies room in a restroom stall crying because I just couldn't take seeing you the way you were and most of all seeing you with her. I feel in so many ways she is not right for you and don't know how to love you like a real woman should.

It's so crazy because just as I was able to pull myself together and leave the stall, Rozalyn came through the door crying very emotional tears as well. I don't know what I was thinking but I just climbed onto the toilet and just listened to her cry. Honestly I don't know what I thought I would hear or find out but I just sat there and waited. Waited to see if maybe she could give me some information that would destroy your relationship with her. Please don't think that I do not want to see you happy but I just know she isn't the one for you and I couldn't have been more than right.

After getting into a blowout with her little home girls, some dude came into the restroom. At first I believed it to be you until I heard him speak. They had a few words and then suddenly I heard moaning, Tae. They were having sex; through the cracks of the stall I could see them passionately involved with each other like it wasn't their first time. And after it was all over she started accusing this guy of rape and screaming for help. I'm not sure who this guy was but only could see that he was light skinned and about six feet tall.

I wanted to come out of that stall and scream that she was lying about what happened but it was not the time or the place. I'm sorry that I am even coming to you like this but I felt in my heart that you needed to know. I hope to hear from you as soon as possible. Take care.

Love,

Kari

After losing my two best friends, escaping some serious jail time, and getting out the dope game alive and wealthy; I've learned to appreciate life and those that I have around me. Having my son Tamarion in my life, a son that I thought I almost lost and my other two sons Zavier and Zyir has made me rethink my entire life.

Cheating and beating on their mom is something that I truly regret and have been feeling fucked up over for a long time. I grew up watching my pops do the same shit to my moms and I hated him for it. That is exactly what I didn't want from my sons; for them to hate me. I wanted them to respect me as a man, as their father, their provider, and as the man that loved their moms.

Vacationing in Puerto Rico made me more than certain that I loved my wife Rozalyn, she is everything to me. Over these last few months all I could think about was righting my wrongs with her. Forgetting about all the bullshit we've been through, the mistakes we've both made and move on. All I want to do is care for Rozalyn, grow old with her, and build a strong foundation with her; something that my parents never had.

Arriving back in Miami I was so fucking ready to get back to a brand new life with my family. Now, as soon as I open my mail I come home to this bullshit letter informing me that the foundation I was trying to build was worthless. My fuckin' wife was a worthless piece of shit. For her to lie to me and say that Brandon raped her at Keylan's wake was an all-time low. To willingly fuck Brandon in the restroom at a wake was disrespectful as hell and I couldn't just let it go.

Tae, somebody is at the gate trying to get in," Rozalyn said.

I heard her speaking but all I could think of was if I should do what I was thinking of doing. If I let her get away with this shit, how could I be sure she wouldn't do it again? No, fuck all that. How can I even look at her the same after the bullshit she did?

"Tamar, Danesha is at the gate!" She yelled. "Tamar!"

I looked down at the letter once more hoping that the words I read would change and somehow I would read something different than before.

"Rozalyn, I've gotten my life together and I wanna take my baby girl home," Danesha said sympathetically over the intercom.

She released the button on the speaker, turned around, and stood face to face with me. Before any words could fly from her mouth I grabbed her by the throat and began to snatch her useless ass life away.

"You wanna tell me what the fuck really went on in that restroom the day of Keylan's wake?" I asked gripping her neck tighter and tighter.

Her skin became flushed as all the color began to leave her. Her eyes pleaded with me to let her go but I just couldn't. She has played me too many times and this was going to be the last time.

BLAM!

My knees went limp causing me to lose my grip around Rozalyn's neck and fall over. Her body collapsed to the floor while she frantically let out long, dry, heaving noises.

"I dare you to put your damn hands on me! You just like your no good daddy! Have you lost your damn mind Tae?" my moms asked as she stood over me with only the cord in her hand from the broken lamp she'd hit me with.

"Mommy!" my son Tamarion yelled as he ran into the room to his mama's side.

"You fuckin' lucky right now she came when she did! I want you to pack your shit up and get the fuck outta my house you dumb bitch!" I bellowed at Rozalyn.

"What? What are you talking about? She isn't going anywhere," my moms said.

"Look mama stay out of this! Unless you want this bitch dead I suggest you help her pack her shit! I want her outta of here by the time I come back, and leave my fuckin' kids here bitch!"

Hurriedly I left out of the room, down the stairs and out of the house. The headlights from a car could be seen down the long driveway and suddenly I remembered that Diamond's bitch ass was trying to get in. I hopped in my truck, cranked it, and sped down the driveway. Somebody was gonna get murdered tonight and if it wasn't going to be Rozalyn then Diamond would be a good replacement.

EERCCHHHH!

Jumping out of my truck, I walked over to the security booth and punched the code into the gate. I leaned up against the door and waited for Diamond to drive in. She was a fool if she thought that my heart was forgiving like her sister's was. Soon as the tail end of Diamond's car pulled in, I pressed the button to securely close the gate back then stepped out of the booth. My car was keeping her from going too far. She rolled her passenger side window down and lowered her head so that she could make eye contact with me.

"Hey Tae, did Roz tell you why I..." she started to say but the two bullets I sent into her skull quickly shut her up. All this time this bitch hadn't been thinking about her baby and now all of a sudden she wants to pop up talking about she got her life together and wants her back. I pulled out my cell and dialed my brother Taron's number. Now that I no longer had Keylan or Brandon, Taron was the only somebody I could call on right now. I asked Taron to meet me in thirty minutes at the club we owned downtown. I walked back to the security gate pushing the button to open the gate back up then ran over to Diamond's car. I pushed her body to the side then took her place in the seat before peeling out of the gate before it closed. I was well aware that everything I'd just done was caught on my security system but I didn't care. My moms knew what kind of man I grew up to be and Rozalyn damn well knew what kind of man she married. Her ass just better be lucky it wasn't her that died tonight.

1: Rozalyn

1 year later....

"Mrs. Andrews, I want to commend you on your progress thus far. I see that you've been maintaining a successful business for the past four months and just recently purchased a home. I also see that you're attending school. This is a whole lot better from eight months ago," the judge said never taking his stare away from me.

I sat behind the defendants table, fidgeting like crazy. I'd worked so hard over the past year to get where I am today.

I smiled on the inside as satisfaction crossed over me. I was finally doing something that made me happy, made me proud, and others proud of me as well. Two months ago, I moved out of my brother Kevin's house and into my own; yes, my shit. Tamar and I are no longer together and for the first time ever; I didn't give a fuck.

Yea, I was a fucking fool behind that muthafucka. He'd had so much mind control over my ass that I never realized how poisonous our relationship was. Not only was it poisonous but violent and crazy as hell. It took him damn near choking me to death and killing my sister in the drive-way of our home for me to realize he wasn't for me.

I've suffered some since leaving Tamar, for one, my lifestyle is nowhere near as lavish as it was when I was with him. Two, I've been going through a custody battle with him ever since the day we split. He currently has custody of the boys and I have no parental rights at all. The court declared that I wasn't fit to be a mother to them due to me not having an education, a job, and two suicide attempts on record.

All I could say is that money talks and he definitely paid for that shit to happen. They did so much looking into my background that they didn't care to even flip a page in his.

The last straw that broke the camel's back was when the state came and took my niece Shanya away from me. After they found out I lost custody of the boys; it was a wrap for me. I'd completely lost my whole family and honestly that shit hurt like hell but I didn't let it destroy me.

Getting my life together was my number one priority; it was the only way I would get to spend even a minute with my boys. I earned my GED through a four week program, and enrolled in college shortly after. I'm only ten credits away from receiving my associates degree in Criminal Justice and planning to go back to get a bachelor's. I've always wanted to be a lawyer and since I'm still young, I have time.

After getting tired of living off my brother and hearing him and his fiancé Kayla aka Ki-Ki fight all the time, I decided I needed a job. Going out on a limb, opening a beauty shop came to mind and my brother helped me to make it happen. Not once did I think I would have what it took to successfully run a business but after being open for just four months; business is booming and my shop is rated number three in the state.

The money is way better than I'd ever expected, especially being I wasn't much of a stylist. I could braid my ass off but that was about it. I had six other stylists working for me and my best friend Brian was one of them.

We did everything from make-up, to hair and nails, and massages. Being a beauty shop owner isn't and wasn't one of my dreams but it did provide me with a comfortable lifestyle to get to where I wanted and needed to be.

Everything I've done was for today, to gain back custody of my boys and prove to Tamar that I can be somebody without him.

The judge cleared his throat before speaking again, "Although, you've made a great deal of improvement. I think it's best that the children stay in the custody of their father."

My whole world came crashing down, this shit just can't be right. I've done everything possible to prove that I can be a good mother and provide for my boys. I don't even know the last time I've had a good night's sleep 'cause I'm always on the grind. I've been hustlin' so hard to get my shit straight and it didn't seem to matter. This judge just had to be on Tamar's payroll, he just had to be.

Doing my best to stifle my cries, I held my head down into my chest. It seemed that no matter what I did, Tamar would always win.

"Your honor, with the improvements that Rozalyn has made; is it at least possible that she gets visitation?" my lawyer Greg posed the question.

"Yes," the judge stated flatly.

That got me to lift my head up. Something was way better than nothing. The judge removed his thick glasses, rubbed his eyes, and then put them back on.

"After careful consideration, I am in agreement that visitation rights are deserved. I'm ordering a standard visitation order to take effective immediately. Mr. Andrews is to make sure the children are available this Friday at seven p.m., and Mrs. Andrews you are to have them back no later than 6:30 p.m. Sunday evening."

You couldn't stop the smile that lit up across my face. My tears of pain suddenly became tears of joy. In just three more days I would finally get to see my boys again. I glanced over at Tamar who was notably pissed. I don't know why he got such great satisfaction out of keeping my kids away from me and going through this has truly made me realize how dumb I was.

"Where are we on the divorce proceedings?" the judge asked looking from my lawyer to Tamar's.

Greg stood up, "Rozalyn has been showing up once a week to appointed counseling sessions but Mr. Andrews has been a no show each time."

"Mmph," the judge sighed. I'm sure he was thinking the same thing I'd been thinking all this time. For someone who claimed that they wanted nothing to do with me, and how I was a nasty project bitch, who wasn't going to amount to shit in life; he couldn't seem to let me go.

He filed for a divorce months ago but doesn't want to do what it takes to finalize it. The judge ordered that we complete thirty two hours of therapy with a marriage counselor. He said that young people got married at the drop of a dime and never did what it took to stay married. He wanted to ensure that there wasn't any way possible that we would want to reconcile.

I don't know about Tamar but I knew for certain I was done and was more than ready to get this divorce under wraps.

"I'm giving sixty days from today's date to get the counseling ordered completed. If it is not completed at that time the proceedings will be closed out and the process will have to be restarted. Am I clear?" the judge asked.

I nodded my head and looked towards Tamar; he rubbed his goatee, seemingly in deep thought. This was the first time I'd seen him in eight months; since our last court meeting and I must admit he was looking dapper. Better than I remembered. The judge set our next court date and dismissed us until that time.

Eagerly I arose from my chair and wrapped my arms around my attorney Greg. It had cost me a pretty penny to retain him and so far it seemed worth it. I would pay him every last dime I had if it meant I would regain custody of my children.

"Aaghhh!" I screamed and jumped into Brian's arms. He showed signs that he'd been crying and I could see that he was happy for me. He'd listened to me complain daily about my situation and now we finally had something to celebrate.

Brian and I walked out of the court room together smiling from ear to ear, but my smile quickly faded upon seeing

Tamar's new girlfriend. It was that reporter bitch Kari, the one that sent Tamar all those naked pictures when he and I were together. I hated bitches like her, she was waiting in the trenches for me to fuck up and when I did, she jumped on Tamar's dick so fast; my juices didn't even get a chance to dry up.

"Bitch," I said noticing she was staring at me behind her big ass Dior sunglasses.

"Hi little girl. How are you?" she asked before removing her glasses.

"Brian, let's go," I grabbed his hand and trotted down the stairs.

"Roz!" Tamar called after me.

I stopped in my tracks and turned to see him and Kari holding hands as they made their way in my direction. I placed one hand on my hip waiting for them to get closer. I didn't have anything to say to Tamar or Kari's ass, all I needed was for him to have Tamarion, Zyir, and Zavier ready for me on Friday.

"Yea," I said with a hint of attitude.

"I'll have Taron bring the boys over to you on Friday. Go ahead and set up that counseling shit and let me know---"

I cut him off, "It's already set up, same day and time every week. Just make sure you don't waste my time once again and not show up."

I didn't miss Tamar's eyes as they cut across my body. He licked his lips when he made it down to my hips. I smirked at his ass then turned to leave once again.

"Damn, did he just mind fuck you?" Brian asked through laughter.

"Hell yea, I saw that shit too!" I laughed.

"Bitch, I am so happy for you! We celebrating tonight! Drinks on me and yes I am getting you very fucked up!"

I grabbed Brian's hand and squeezed it tightly, "I can't wait. Oh my God! I can't wait!"

We headed towards my new Jeep Liberty and was about to get in when we heard the deafening sounds of an explosion. The force of the explosion pushed me forward and caused me to hit the door of my car with a thud.

Brian scattered across the ground towards me, there was blood dripping from his nose and a few scratches across his face.

"You okay?" he asked helping me to my feet.

"Yea, are you? What the fuck was that?" I asked wiping debris from my clothing.

"Shit, look," Brian's eyes shot across the parking lot.

A handful of people laid out on the pavement and two of them just so happen to be Tamar and Kari. Tamar's black Navigator sat in flames, melting the metal away by the minute. I tried to run towards them when a second explosion halted me and threw me back towards the ground.

"Oh my God, Tamar!" I cried.

His truck literally lifted from the ground as more flames surrounded it. Leaping to my feet, I jolted across the parking lot towards Tamar, and grabbed him by his arms. Seeing him like this reminded me of the time he was shot up in his trap house; body leaking with blood from the many bullets that penetrated his skin. It was the incident that started a whole whirlwind of madness.

"Rozalyn, you gotta get back! Get back before this shit blows the hell up again," Brian wrapped his arm around me and pulled me away from Tamar.

I wanted to help Tamar and I didn't understand why. He's put me through hell for a year, took my kids from me, caused my niece to be taken away and treated me worse than dog shit. Why the fuck did I want to help him?

I stared at Tamar's limp body as I backed away from the scene.

"Fuck!" I yelled out. I grabbed my purse and threw everything that fell out back into it. Brian and I jumped into my jeep and peeled away from the lot. A thousand thoughts ran through my head, thoughts that confused the hell out of me.

I wanted to go back, my heart kept telling me to go back, but my mind kept telling me fuck that nigga and let his new bitch worry about him. Yea, fuck him and let the new boo worry 'bout that ass.

***

I stormed through the doors of my beauty shop, not saying hello or excuse me to anyone. Rushing towards the back of the building, I stuck my key in the lock of my office, rushed in and slammed the door behind me. I threw everything in my hands across the room making loud crashing noises.

Tears rushed from my face but I shook my head quickly to prevent them from falling. I didn't know why I was feeling this way or why was I scared as fuck right now. The fluttering of my heart told me I still had feelings for Tamar. Feelings I had no business having.

"Rozalyn, get yourself together. Damn," Brian said after coming into my office. "Why are you crying?"

"Brian, he could be dead and I left him there!" I yelled.

"He ain't your responsibility anymore. Are you serious right now?"

"I don't know why I care Brian. I don't get it. What is wrong with me?"

"I don't know, maybe you're dumb, stupid, desperate," Brian ran his fingers through his dreads and leaned against my desk.

"Brian---" I started but was cut off.

"That's what you acting like. Look, get yourself together because there are a shit load of customers waiting to be serviced. You know I don't give a fuck about Tae, so you gets no love from me," Brian rolled his eyes and left my office.

I walked around and sat in the chair behind my desk, grabbing a mirror from the drawer; I looked over my face. My eyes were red and my mascara was running. I picked up the phone to dial my brother Kevin's number. I had to find a way to inconspicuously check on Tamar.

"What up?" Kevin asked. "How did everything go?"

"I didn't get custody back but I did get visitation," I said into the receiver.

"That's what's up lil' sis. So, when do you get to see them?"

"This Friday, I cannot wait. I bet Tamarion is so big and oh my God the twins, I haven't seen them since they were five months old. They not even gonna know me," I said and instantly felt nervous.

It never dawned on me that my kids most likely didn't remember me. It has been forever since I've seen them and since Kari is around all the time; I'm sure they believe she's their mama. Just the thought of that made me sick.

"Hold on real quick Roz, let me get this other line," Kevin said snapping me from my thoughts.

"Yea okay," I sighed. I'd called Kevin to see what he knew about Tamar and if nothing to see what he could find out. The conversation took an indirect turn and had me feeling some type of way.

Everyday I've complained about my boys not being with me and now I'm having second thoughts. Fear of rejection crippled my judgment and got me to believing that they were better off where they are.

"Aye," Kevin came back to the line not sounding like he did before he clicked over. "Tae, in the hospital. Ron said they don't know if he's gonna make it."

A ringing in my ears kept me from hearing anything further. The phone dropped from my hand onto the floor, crashing into pieces once it made contact with the tiled floor.

This isn't at all what I wanted. Even if my life could possibly get easier, I didn't want Tamar dead. Regardless of what he's done to me and how he's treated me; I would never want to see him dead.

I grabbed my car keys and my purse and raced out of my office. Only thing I could see at this point was Tamar lying out on the pavement after his car exploded into tiny pieces. All I could remember is how I drove away and left him there to possibly burn away like an unwanted piece of trash.

"Rozalyn! Roz!" Brian called after me.

Nothing mattered to me at this moment. All I knew is that I needed to get to the hospital to see Tamar. As I got into my car my mind began playing tricks on me again and seeing Brian peering through my tinted windows partially confirmed that I was once again being a fool. How the hell would I look showing up to the hospital after the hell this boy has put me through?

But I am still his wife. I considered.

But he has a girlfriend, a girlfriend that lives with him. I reasoned.

He also has kept my kids away from me for a fuckin' year. What dumb bitch still cares about a nigga that does that? I concluded.

After careful consideration, I opened the door to my car, shook my head, and walked back into my shop. I had three appointments lined up for the remainder of the day, money to be made, and shit to take care of. All I could do is hope and pray that the fool would be okay; hell he was no longer my concern.

"What the hell is going on? Are you okay?" Brian asked.

"I'm good. I just had a moment but I'm good. Let's just get this day started and over with," I said and walked over to my chair and began to set up all my equipment. I had to remember that Tamar was no longer my concern, the same as I wasn't his.

2:Rozalyn

BAM! BAM! BAM!

Ding Dong! Ding Dong!

"Who is it?" I sighed, pulling my robe tightly closed. I looked out the window of my front door and noticed Taron standing on the other side holding my boys in his hand. A big smile crept on my face as I quickly undid the locks and pulled the door open. "Oh my God!"

"Shh, I just got them to go to sleep. Go and get Zyir out the back seat," Taron said as he moved his way into the house.

I rushed outside to Taron's Ford F-150 and pulled the back door open. Zyir was laid across the back seat, looking like a replica of my big brother Zavier. I picked him up, placed him over my shoulder, and took him into my home. I'd already gotten their bedroom together when I first moved here; each of them had their own bed with cartoon character themed blankets. This visit from Taron was truly a surprise being that I wasn't supposed to get them until this Friday evening.

I lay Zyir in his bed, pulled off his shoes and socks and placed him underneath the covers. I couldn't help but stare down at all of my boys, gloating over how big they'd grown since I'd last seen them. Tears suddenly crept down my face as I watched the three of them and couldn't believe that I'd created three beautiful little boys that would one day grow up and become great men.

"I need to holla at you," Taron said.

"Okay," I said wiping my face. I gave each of them a kiss, turned off the light in the bedroom, and followed Taron to my living room.

Taron wore a mug across his face that said that what he had to talk to me about wasn't going to be good. Defensively, I placed my hands on my hip and waited for him to say whatever he had to say. He took in a deep breath, took a seat on the edge of sofa, and then looked up at me with tears in his eyes. Quickly I softened, lowered my hands, and walked closer to him.

"What's the matter?" I asked.

"Tamar is fucked up. They finally stopped the internal bleeding a couple of hours ago and stabilized him. I almost lost my only fuckin' brother and your ass wasn't there!" Taron yelled. His expression turned from sad to anger in a matter of seconds.

"Taron I—"

"I don't wanna hear shit Roz! You were supposed to be there for him! That's your damn husband!"

"My husband?" I questioned him. "My husband has put me through hell, doing everything to keep our children from me for a damn year and you wanna talk to me about being there for him?"

"Look, I ain't saying that Tamar was right in any of the shit he was doing. I told him damn near everyday how wrong he was from keeping the boys away from you but you know how he is. Rozalyn, you hurt him and that was how he coped. That nigga still cares for you and I think you of all people know that and you should've been there for him."

I couldn't help but laugh at how Taron was making his poor little brother out to be the victim. Yea I know I fucked up and violated the code when I slept with his homeboy but Tamar has done so many things to me that it wasn't even funny. He beat my ass silly so many times, gave me a STD, and tried to blame the shit on me, slept with my sister, and so much other shit. I couldn't believe Taron had the nerve to sit up here and say that Tamar was hurt.

"I understand that's your brother and everything but we're no longer together. I hate that he's in the hospital and struggling to survive right now but that's not my problem. He's with Kari and that's who needs to be worried about whether he lives or dies right now. Not me," I said pointing my finger into my chest.

"What? Are you fuckin' serious? You're gonna let this childish ass bullshit keep you from standing by my brother's side?" Taron questioned in disbelief.

"Taron thank you for bringing my children to me. I will take very good care of them but it's time for you to leave", I said and crossed my arms over my chest.

"So you're not coming to the hospital?" Taron asked as he stood up.

"Nope," I said flatly.

"Just want you to know that that's fucked up. I'll be sure to let Tamar know that you don't give a fuck."

I shrugged my shoulders and walked behind Taron as he exited out of the door. I locked the door then went into my bedroom pulling my covers off of the bed. I went into the boys' room and spread my covers onto the floor and lay down to go to sleep. I couldn't wait until the morning to see my boys smiling faces. Once again Tamar was that other bitch's problem; not mine.

***

The boys woke up crying and scared the next morning. It took forever to get them to quiet down and even let me come near them. In the beginning, Tamarion shied away but eventually he came around and called me mama. Now the twins, they didn't want anything to do with me, didn't want me talking to them, or even touching them.

It took everything in me not to cry, not to be mad, and sad that my own kids didn't even know who the hell I was. I kept telling myself to just be happy that I finally got to see them again and eventually they will know who I am.

"I don't know what the hell I was thinking bringing three kids to the grocery store," I mumbled as I picked up a box of fruit snacks that Zyir had thrown to the floor.

"No!" he yelled and slapped my hand as I tried to place it back on the shelf.

I looked down at him like he was crazy then looked around to see if anyone was looking before I popped him on his hand.

"Don't you tell me no!" I said.

He started yelling and screaming, and falling out on the floor like I'd killed him. His brother's ran in circles around him as they laughed and pointed.

"Oh my God," I said shaking my head. "Okay, stop it!"

I picked Zyir up and placed him in the basket, once I turned around Tamarion and Zavier took off running down the aisle.

"No! Zavier and Zyir!" I yelled.

I pushed the basket and had to chase behind them. I couldn't believe this shit was happening to me right now. I remember how I used to laugh and say how I wasn't going to be one of those mothers that couldn't control their kids in public, but look at me now. I've only been able to pick up three damn items on my list and was nowhere near done.

"Slow down, slow down before y'all fall and bust ya' head."

"I'm so sorry," I said grabbing Zavier and putting him in the basket.

"It's cool. They have a lot of energy is all," the stranger said with his accent thick. He put Tamarion in the front of the basket and then gave each of them a five.

"Thank You," I sighed.

"Already. I'm Messiah pretty lady. What's your name?"

"Look I appreciate it but I need to hurry up and finish before they go crazy on me. Thanks again," I pushed the basket away but stopped when he pulled my grocery list from my hand. "What the---"

"Let me help you out. Cheese, bread, milk---"

"Are you fuckin' serious right now?" I asked with one hand on my hip.

Damn I must admit that dude was kinda sexy. I thought noticing his sexy hazel eyes, light brown skin, and sexy full lips. He was about five-nine and maybe a good buck fifty.

"I'm trying to help you. You already got your hands full so let me grab what you need and you push the basket," he said with a smirk.

I couldn't help but laugh as I contemplated his offer, I knew without the help I would be in here for hours. I nodded my head and pushed the basket along while Mr. Messiah grabbed things from my list.

"So, are these your lil' brothers?" Messiah asked while placing two cans of chili in the basket.

"No, these are my kids," I answered. "Put your hand back in the basket Zyir."

"You don't look old enough to have any kids ma'. You don't even look like you had kids. How old are you?"

"I'll be twenty in a few months."

"That's what's up? You from around here? I've never seen you before today."

"I'm from Atlanta, well Brooklyn, New York. I've only been out here for a few years."

"Yea I knew I heard that Brooklyn flava coming from you when you speak," he laughed.

"I ain't the only one speaking with an accent," I looked up at him.

"Yea, I'm from the Virgin Islands but I've been living in Miami for the past seven or eight years now."

I nodded my head and grabbed a box of cookies from the basket, opening them quickly and handing one to each of the boys.

"Cookies!" Tamarion yelled out.

"Are you gonna tell me your name or do I have to keep calling you pretty lady. I mean I don't mind--"

"My name is Rozalyn," I smiled.

"Rozalyn. Rozalyn. Rozalyn."

I shook my head and continued shopping only giving vague answers to all the questions that Messiah was asking. I couldn't help but blush, the man had taken time out his day to help me do my shopping and it was very flattering.

Once we'd gotten everything and got into the line to check out, Messiah reached into his pocket and pulled out a knot full of money. He handed a few bills over to the cashier before I could even get my money out.

"What are you doing?" I asked.

He shrugged his shoulders, "What your man should've been doing."

"Well I don't need you to do that. I got money to pay for it myself," I said with anger. I reached into my purse, fishing around for my wallet but couldn't find it. After checking and rechecking and still not coming up with it, I then remembered I took it out last night when paying bills. I held my head down feeling grateful and embarrassed at the same time.

Messiah grabbed the change from the cashier then began to push the basket outside of the store. Once we reached the jeep, he put the groceries in the back, and assisted with strapping the boys down.

"I left my wallet at home and uh--"

"You don't have to explain anything to me. It was only a few hundred dollars and it's plenty more where that came from," Messiah said with a smirk.

"Well, I want to pay you back. I don't really like idea of you paying for my groceries and shit."

"Just give me your number and I'll call you tomorrow or something, you can give it to me then," Messiah took out his cell phone punching in numbers as I called out them out.

We both said our goodbyes and left.

3: Tamar

My whole body ached with pain from being tossed in the air from the explosion of my car. Metal parts and glass pierced through my legs and caused internal bleeding that almost killed me. My legs were numb, weak, and I pretty much couldn't move them. Doctors informed me that I would have to go through therapy to strengthen them again which was cool. I'm just glad that I hadn't been paralyzed or even worse; dead. If it had not been for the remote starter installed on my truck the situation could've been a lot worse.

Kari hadn't been hurt too bad and checked out of the hospital a couple of days ago. We'd been dating for about eight months now, after leaving her husband and filing for a divorce she moved in with me. She's been real good with the boys and things have been going real good between us. She honestly has been a key factor in me keeping my mind off of Rozalyn.

When I received that letter from Kari telling me what she witnessed in the bathroom at Keylan's wake, it really messed my damn head up. I ain't never felt so much hurt in my damn life. I've been betrayed by my blood, damn near killed by my cousin at the orders of my father, and none of that shit compared to what Rozalyn did to me.

She can blame it all on me being in a relationship with Danesha, her sister, if she wants to but that shit is irrelevant. I knew nothing about Rozalyn's past besides the fact she moved from New York from her mom's to Atlanta to live with her dad. I had never seen her mama or her sister a day in damn my life. And the fact that them hoes was like day and night didn't help. Danesha was fully black and Rozalyn's ass was mixed with black and some more shit.

Instead of her understanding the mistake I made she goes and violate the ultimate code and fucked my ex best friend. Rozalyn better be glad my mama saved her ass that night 'cause she would've been buried right along with her sister. Fuckin' slut!

The shit that really threw me for a loop is the fact that I'm sitting in my hospital bed, face all scrunched up as my brother Taron sits here telling me how nonchalant Rozalyn has been acting about me damn near dying. A whole week I've been here and the bitch didn't even step foot in the hospital.

Why is this fucking with me? I wondered to myself tossing ice chips down my mouth.

"I gotta give it to shorty though, her shop making noise all over Miami though," Taron said.

"Good for her, I really don't give a fuck," I said.

"Got a nice lil' house tucked off in a nice neighborhood, brand new jeep sitting in the driveway. Rozalyn showed up and showed out. I'm proud of her," Taron smirked.

I looked at him sideways, reached in my cup, and took a piece of ice out, throwing it his way. I shook my head and adjusted the pillow.

"Stop trying to act like you don't care though bruh. You did all this shit to try and avoid her, took her through hell, and now you pissed that she don't care no more."

"I'm not tripping off that. I'm pissed at the fact the bitch got my kids longer than what she was supposed to."

"They good. I've been checking on them every day. What we need to be worried about is who did this shit to you," Taron said scooting his chair closer to me.

"Who knows man? I exited the game a rich nigga then got back in and started hurting these fools' pockets all over again. It could be anybody at this point," I answered honestly.

I had every intention of retiring and staying out the game for good but that was when I had my family. When Rozalyn and I separated, I needed something to keep me busy and to keep my mind off of killing her. The dope game always gave me the kinda distraction I needed to keep my mind off of bullshit. At the end of the day, no matter the reason I went back in; the dope game was severely suffering without me.

From Atlanta to Miami, no one had a connect good enough to feed the cities sufficiently. Streets began to dry up, dope boys pockets began to dwindle, and the crime rate went up quickly. I got back up with Dmitri and his pops and within a month I successfully pulled in over 2.5 million dollars. Fuck the bullshit. Selling dope was my calling. Of course it didn't feel the same without my right and my left being by my side. With Keylan being dead and Brandon locked away in a mental asylum, it really didn't feel the same.

I still had my brother Taron and now Rozalyn's brother Kevin but I would give anything to turn back the hands of time and have my boys with me. Til' this day it hurt to think about the way shit went down with all of us. I should've never beat Brandon's ass damn near to death the way I did, and I should've never set Brandon up to be killed which in turn ended in Keylan's death. Before, I placed the blame on everybody else but it wasn't anybody's fault but my own. It was wrong to blame Rozalyn for fucking my boy and blaming Keylan for not putting Brandon down when he had the chance was the wrong thing to do too. We've been boys too long and everything should've been handled differently.

It wasn't anything that could be done now, I had to accept the fact that what we had for years will never be again. Looking forward is all I can do at this point.

"Did Dmitri talk to you about using this club for a coming home party for some cat he knows?" Taron asked breaking my thoughts.

"Nah, he ain't said anything about it. Who is it for?" I asked.

"I can't remember dude name. Did three years in the penn for some drug charges, dude was supposed to be a big deal around here at one point."

I shrugged my shoulders, "Is it gonna bring in some money? Dmitri knows the deal. Guarantee the door and the bar gets its minimum and I'm cool with it."

"I'll let him know. I guess I'll go through here and check on--"

"*Knock, knock!*"

I looked towards the door to see Rozalyn peeking around the corner. The boys came running in full speed towards my bed.

"Sup big man!" I said giving Tamarion a five and reaching over to pull him in the bed.

"Sup daddy," he said giggling.

"Daddy chilling just trying to get better so I can come home. Miss y'all," I said tickling him until he couldn't take it any longer.

I nodded my head at Rozalyn who continued to stand by the door like a stranger. She looked good wearing her hair down and curly, with a simple black dress that hugged her small frame.

"Zavier, Zyir, y'all not gonna come speak to me," I said holding my arms out for the twins.

"They look like they mad about something," Taron said as he walked over and picked up Zyir and Zavier bringing them over to me.

"They just woke up," Rozalyn said now focusing on her cell phone.

"You know you can bring your ass in the room. Nice of you to finally make a fuckin' appearance," I said voice filling with anger.

"I didn't come up here for you. I just stopped by so the boys can visit since they've been asking about you. I'm going to the waiting room, just let me know when they're ready to go," Rozalyn turned to walk away.

"Rozalyn!" Taron called after her.

"Nah, let that bitch go," I spat.

"Chill on that bitch shit in front of your shorties bruh. Told you that shit before. Don't do that," Taron said and left out of the room behind Rozalyn.

I shook my head trying to take my mind off Rozalyn. I couldn't believe that we'd gotten to the point where she didn't even wanna be in the same room as me. As much as I attempted to let it roll off my back and concentrate on chilling with my boys; I couldn't. I still had love for her and it was really starting to show.

4: Rozalyn

I sat on the patio of Razoos Cajun restaurant sipping on a sprite and looking over the menu. Tamar was still in the hospital and I still had the boys which was cool with me. Every day they were getting more and more used to me and feeling more comfortable around me. I took on fewer appointments at the shop since I had them full time just so that I could spend as much time with them as possible.

"Are you ready to order yet?" the waiter asked.

"No, not yet. I'm waiting for someone," I smiled.

"And I'm here," I looked up and saw Messiah standing over me looking spiffy in a crisp white t-shirt, a pair of True Religion jeans, and black and red J's. His mini fro was manicured well with a fresh line up.

"Hey," I stood up to greet him, giving a quick hug as he pecked me on my cheek.

"Smell good," he said in his thick accent. He took a seat across from me and shot a gorgeous smile in my direction.

"Smell like hair spray and shampoo," I giggled. "I haven't ordered yet. Have you been here before?"

"I've been here once. Only for drinks though that was back before I got locked up," Messiah said looking over the menu.

I looked at Messiah wearily wondering why this was the first time I'd heard about him being locked up. We've spoken on the phone numerous times since the day at the grocery store and even stayed up late texting back and forth and this is the first I'm hearing this.

"Locked up?" I asked seeing as how he wasn't going to elaborate.

"Yea, I did three years in the penitentiary after I got caught with some dope and a gun. Nothing major, I took my charge and served my time", Messiah shrugged.

"Oh wow," I said really unsure what to say next.

"Yea, I'm a felon. Does that bother you?" Messiah placed his menu down and eyed me seriously.

"No--I---I just didn't know is all. Your past is your past. I won't judge you," I said.

Once the waiter came I ordered the stuff'd fish and Messiah ordered the stuff'd shrimp. While waiting for our food we discussed everything from Messiah's upbringing in the Virgin Islands to his life in Miami. He talked about some of the things he went through while locked up and how he had to pray every day that he didn't kill a nigga up in there. Just sitting here and listening to Messiah openly discuss some things that others may have kept private gave me a lot of respect for him.

He kinda had me rethinking my no dating policy while I was still married. Seeing as how Tamar isn't cooperating and doing what's needed to finalize the divorce; I'll be married forever. I couldn't allow him to continue to control my life over a few counseling sessions that he most likely would never attend. Messiah seemed like an interesting dude and I honestly wanted to know more.

"Lunch was good. I wanna take you to dinner, breakfast, shopping--hell I just wanna be in your presence more," Messiah said as the waiter took our plates away.

"I had a good time as well and yes we should do this again," I smiled.

"That's what's up. We gonna have to get together real soon. You about to go back to work?" Messiah asked.

He tossed a twenty dollar tip on the table and stood up along with me. We walked off the patio dining area and towards my car.

"Yea, I have one more appointment before I can go to pick my boys up."

"Cool, cool. Well hit me up later once you get home and get settled," Messiah leaned over and kissed me on my lips. He wrapped his arms around my waist and slid his tongue into my mouth.

"Damn," I said when we finally pulled away.

Messiah gave me another peck on the lips, then bit down on his bottom as he backed away from me.

"Damn," I said once again then got into my car to leave.

****

Once I made it to the shop, I noticed a tall, slender female standing out front. She was light skinned with freckles wearing a pair of thin glasses. Her hair was pinned up in a bun and her edges were a hot ass mess. I figured she was here waiting on one of my stylist until I got closer and noticed just who she was.

"Kari?" I questioned once I got closer.

I guess I should've known who she was just by looking at her body but then again the bitch wasn't naked. She sent so many naked pictures to Tamar while we were together that I bet I know that hoes body better than I know my own.

"Rozalyn, hi. Do you have a few minutes? I need to speak with you," Kari folded her arms across her chest and shifted her weight to one leg.

She didn't look like she'd just been in an accident or at least recovering from one. I nodded my head at Kari and invited her to follow me inside the shop to my office. Once inside, I signaled for her to sit down. Normally when I had visitors I would offer them juice, water, or coffee but the bitch's visit was unwarranted. The hoe ruined my marriage and honestly I didn't see the need to be courteous.

"What's up?" I asked sitting behind my desk.

"Look congrats to you on getting your kids back and all that. I just wanted to warn you that Tamar and I getting married pretty soon and I would appreciate it if you didn't get in the way of that," Kari flashed a nice sized diamond on her finger and smirked.

I laughed, "Congrats Kari. I honestly don't give a damn what you and Tamar are about to do. You both have my best wishes. Long as he don't try and keep me away from my kids again then we won't have any problems."

"So you say. I will see to it that he doesn't fight the custody battle any further and I would appreciate it if you would go ahead and agree to the terms of the divorce so that we can move forward with our lives. And if you don't care then why are you holding up the process?"

"What are you talking about Kari? I'm not holding up anything. All Tamar needs to do is show up for the counseling sessions and this can be over. I've signed the papers a long time ago," I said not believing the bitch had the nerve to accuse me of holding up the divorce proceedings. "Maybe if you start showing up in court next to your man then you will know that. Or wait, does Tamar make you wait outside for him?"

"All I know is that you're keeping us from moving forward and I don't appreciate it. Tamar is mine now. You had your chance and you messed that up when you fucked his best friend. Sign the papers bitch or else the next time you see me it won't be as pleasurable as this one," Kari threatened.

I stood up from my desk and walked around to where Kari sat. I didn't appreciate her coming up in my shop and shooting slugs. Fuck her and Tamar, I was the one showing up week after week to the therapist's office only for Tamar to continuously miss each appointment.

Kari stood from her chair towering over me a good few inches. We stared each other down for what seemed like an eternity before a knock at the door broke our eyes apart.

"Come in," I said.

The door swung open and Brian stood on the other side. He looked Kari up and down and then searched my face for answers.

"Everything good mami?" he asked.

"This bitch was just leaving," I said with a roll of my eyes.

"You heard what I said. Sign the papers bitch," Kari spat before moving around Brian to leave.

"Girl, what the hell was that about?" Brian asked.

"She came up in here talking about her and Tamar getting married and how I need to sign the divorce papers and stop holding them up. Got the nerves to threaten me like I'm supposed to be scared," I huffed parking my behind back in my seat.

"Does the trick not know that Tamar is holding up the process obviously because he still wants you?"

"I don't know what the hell Tamar is telling her but whatever it is it can't be the truth. That's why her ass is always sitting in the waiting area at court. He doesn't want her to know what's going on."

Brian shook his head, "She should've known something was up then. Excuse her for her ignorance. Anyway boo-boo your two o'clock is here."

"Cool, tell her to give me five minutes and I'll be out there."

"Okay," Brian left my office closing the door behind him.

I immediately picked up my office phone, dialed information, and had them transfer me over to the hospital. I waited on the line as the hospital staff rang me into Tamar's room. One thing was for certain, he better get this bitch 'cause she was right. Next time the hoe come at me sideways it won't be pretty.

"Aye, who this?" Tamar answered.

"Look Tamar, you better tell your muthafuckin' fiancé don't come at me with that bullshit again!" I yelled the moment he answered.

"What? Fuck is you talking about?" Tamar asked.

"That bitch Kari came to my damn shop talking about I'm keeping y'all from getting married and if I don't sign the fucking papers it won't be nice the next time she sees me. You better check that hoe and let her know what it really is."

"A'ight Roz," Tamar said and the line went dead.

I hung my office phone up and sat there laughing to myself when suddenly tears fell from my eyes.

Married? That quickly Tamar is getting married. I thought and buried my face into my hands.

****

"Hey Cheryl," I said to Tamar's mother once she opened the door.

"Hey doll, you look tired. Come on in, I just finished dinner and me and the boys were about to sit down and eat. I will fix you a plate," Cheryl ushered me inside, grabbed my hand and led me to the dining area. I wasn't really hungry at all;

pretty much still upset from Kari's visit and didn't feel as if I could stomach anything.

Once I made it into the dining area, all three boys looked at me and smiled before going back to sticking their hands in their food. I walked over to them to assist them with eating. I hated to see them grabbing at the food versus using the silverware that was provided to them.

"So, how have you been Rozalyn? I'm kinda upset that you don't visit with me like you used to. I feel like you shut me out once you and Tamar began having all those problems," Cheryl said and sat a plate in front of me.

"Umm, I probably did shut you out Mrs. Cheryl. I shut everybody out and shut down. It took me a while to get back to my old self again," I answered picking at my food.

"Your old self? Ha, this ain't the old Rozalyn I once knew. You are a woman now doll and I love it on you, looks good."

I laughed, "Thank you. It feels good."

"The boys have been talking about "Mommy" all day. Especially Tamarion, he's been whining for you all day long," Cheryl giggled. "I'm so glad that you and Tamar worked this out and got over that foolishness. I swear that boy is like his father more than he will ever care to admit to."

I nodded my head thinking how Tamar didn't have a choice but to get over his stupidity, the judge forced his hand. It wasn't like he made the decision on his own to allow me to see the boys.

"Aye, mane you do what the fuck you gotta do. Set the test up and let me know when it is," Taron shouted as he walked into the dining area. He walked over and kissed Cheryl on the cheek then took a seat at the table. "Look, I don't care. You not about to have me claiming nothing until I see the proof. Get the fuck off my phone."

Cheryl and I both looked at Taron then at each other. I wondered what that was all about. Taron had been dating a chick for a long while now so hearing him talk about getting a test and claiming something until he had proof baffled me. I know his girlfriend Journey hasn't had a child yet so I wondered what side chick this was.

5: Tamar

"Aaggh!" I groaned as Taron helped me into the house.

"Told you to get a wheel chair hard head," Taron said while he helped me to the family room.

"I don't need no damn wheel chair!"

I pushed his arms off of me and struggled on my own to get to the sofa. My legs felt like they were stuck in cement as I tried to walk the few feet that it took to sit down. After spending a little over a week in the hospital, I'd finally gotten well enough to come home. Regardless of my condition, business was still booming and there were plenty of things that needed to be handled. With me barely trusting anyone, my team was very small and the bulk of the responsibility was mine to take care of.

"Yea, play crazy. You walk like a crippled ass old man," Taron said grabbing the remote, my laptop, and few other gadgets and bringing them to me. "I'm about to go pick up mama, you need anything else?"

I shook my head no and scrolled through my recent call history on my cell phone. "Kari ain't here?"

"I don't know, I wasn't looking for her," Taron shrugged before leaving the room.

I hit the send button when I came across Kari's number. I'd been calling her for a few days trying to talk to her about what Rozalyn told me but hadn't gotten through to her yet.

"Where you at?" I asked the moment she answered.

"Home. How are you?" she asked.

"If you really cared, you would've called me or better yet come to see me. I ain't heard from you since the day this bullshit happened."

"I've just been trying to wrap my head around some things," Kari sighed sounding irritated. "I'm on my way to the hospital, we need to talk."

"Kari, I'm downstairs in the family room. Come holla at me."

I hung up the phone and tossed it to the side. Kari and I were good together but sometimes I often wondered if we jumped in this shit head first. Soon as we started back fooling around and she found out I left Rozalyn for good, she immediately got divorced with the expectations that I would do the same. I had her believing that Rozalyn was the one keeping the divorce from going through and even told her that Rozalyn refused to let me go since I was with her.

Really, the truth was that I wasn't quite ready to close that chapter in my life yet. Although Kari told me what happened in that bathroom at Keylan's wake, I didn't want to believe that Rozalyn would do some foul shit like that to me. Fucking my boy was one thing but to fuck him at the home going celebration of the very nigga he killed was another. The only time I confronted Rozalyn on the issue was when I damn near choked her to death. I haven't brought it to her since then merely because I was too afraid to know the truth.

"How long have you been home?" Kari asked breaking my thoughts.

"I just got here," I replied.

"How are you feeling?" Kari came over to me and kissed me on the lips before sitting down.

"It gets better every day."

I looked over at Kari and couldn't help but notice the tremendous rock sitting on her hand. I immediately frowned being it hadn't been there in all this time we've been together.

"Fuck is this?" I asked grabbing her hand.

"Well seeing as how we always talk about getting married and you have yet to ask I just figured I'd go out and get my own ring," Kari said with a slight smile as she eyed the diamond.

"You the one always talking about getting married, I'm still married Kari. And what's this shit I hear about you going to my wife's--to Rozalyn's shop?"

"I went up there because I'm ready to take that next step Tae! The bitch is--"

I cut her off, "I don't give a fuck what you ready to do! Don't you ever in your life approach her on no bullshit again. Do you understand me?"

"Oh you're defending her now? Before it was this bitch this, or that bitch that. Now you wanna sit here and tell me not to approach her. She is ruining our relationship and you can't even see that."

"Ain't nobody ruining shit for us Kari! I don't give a fuck how you feel about what's going on man; don't do that shit no more! Do not call her; don't go see her, nothing! Stay in your muthafuckin' place!"

"My place? What's my place Tamar? I don't even know what my place is! You tell me that Rozalyn is holding up the process and she tells me otherwise. I'm confused right now."

"If anybody should be confused right now it should be me. Fuck you out shopping for rings and shit while I'm lying up in the hospital for? Forget that other shit, tell me that!"

Kari folded her arms across her chest and looked as if my question caused her to melt away. I've been thinking this whole time she hasn't come to check on me because she was recovering from her damn injuries, but no--she out shopping for rings, and stepping to Rozalyn on some dumb shit.

DING DONG! DING DONG!

"I just wanna get married Tae. I want us to be happy," Kari finally said after moments of silence.

"Man, go get the damn door. Not trying to hear that shit," I said and grabbed my cell phone.

On the screen sat a preview of a picture that was sent from Rozalyn's number. I unlocked my phone and up popped a picture of all three boys smiling from ear to ear. Seeing them so happy made me instantly regret the route I took in keeping them from their moms. I knew what I was doing was wrong but the hurt I felt wouldn't allow me to think reasonably. I just wanted to hurt Rozalyn as much as she hurt me and I didn't care how I went about doing it.

I'm out the hospital but ain't moving around too well. Can you keep them for a couple more weeks?

I hit the send button on the message and sat the phone aside when Dmitri walked in the room followed by a nigga I didn't know. My guards spiked and I rose from my seat barely able to stand. Demitri knew how I felt about muthafuckas I don't know being in my home.

"Fuck is this nigga?" I questioned.

"Chill, this is Sy. The guy I've been telling you about. He's cool people, I've been knowing him for years," Dmitri said holding up his hands.

"Aye Kari!" I yelled ignoring Dmitri's introduction.

"Yea, baby?" Kari stuck her head in the door.

"Go get my muthafuckin' .22. Real quick like," I said fuming that Dmitri brought this cat up in my personal space. I didn't care who this dude was and how long Dmitri had known him.

Dmitri laughed, "Bro chill the hell out. He's good people like I said and as a matter of fact he's going to be working with us."

"Working with who? Fuck is you talking about?" I asked taking a seat back on the sofa.

Kari came into the room and I quickly took the hammer out her hand, cocked it, and sat it on my lap. If nobody knew, Dmitri knew that I had no problems murkin' dude right where he stood. I side eyed the both of them waiting for Dmitri to further explain himself.

"Maybe we should discuss this at another time," Sy said in a thick accent.

Dmitri clicked his tongue before speaking, "Maybe I was wrong for bringing him here without speaking with you first but I vouch for him. He is the kinda cat that you need on your team Tae. If you prefer we will discuss this at a later time but either way it's gonna get discussed; sooner rather than later."

"Hello," I answered my phone when it began to vibrate.

"You know I don't mind keeping my kids you don't have to ask me that," Rozalyn said.

"Our kids," I said giving Dmitri and Sy a menacing look.

"Are you gonna be at the counseling session tomorrow since you're out the hospital?" Rozalyn asked.

"Rozalyn, can't you reschedule it? Damn, I just came home an hour ago," I sighed.

"I've been rescheduling every week for months. It's not like you're doing anything physical. All you have to do is sit there and listen and if you must--talk."

"Reschedule it. I'm not gonna make it," I hung up without waiting for her response. "Look have a seat. Let's get this shit over with."

"Cool," Dmitri said taking a seat next to me. Sy continued to stand but once I placed my grip around the .22 he found a seat near the door.

"What's up?" I inquired.

"Let's start over. Tae, this is Sy, Sy Tae. Sy used to run the West coast down here, real mean on them streets and I know for a fact that he will be crucial to what we got going here. With everything that's going on I think that it would be good to let him eventually take over things here while me and you get things set up in Dallas and Memphis," Demitri laid it all out.

I sat quietly just listening to what Dmitri had to say not giving my input on whether I agreed or disagreed. One thing was for sure, I worked too hard to set up an air tight organization and wasn't about to let anybody take over shit. Especially not somebody I ain't know. Even when I decided to retire I handed things over to my bruh and Kevin, not some niggas I just picked up off the streets.

"Are you listening?" Dmitri asked me.

"Yea I heard everything you said. We can sit down at a later date and time and run through everything. That's a lot to think about you know?" I said knowing I wasn't going to think about shit.

"All I need you to do my man is just show me the ins and outs and I promise you everything you've done will be done just the same if not better," Sy said sounding a tad bit cocky and confident.

"You the one that's trying to throw the party at The Revolver?" I asked changing the subject. I caught the side eye that Dmitri shot at me but ignored him and kept my stare on Sy.

"Yea, Dmitri wanted to throw me a lil' homecoming party and suggested we do it at your spot."

"Ron got back with me this morning and told me we were clear to throw it in a couple of weeks. It's gonna be bananas," Dmitri said. "He never gave me a price though."

"Long as y'all clear the bar and door minimum we cool on that," I shrugged my shoulders.

"Are you gonna come? You and the wifey?" Sy asked like we were long time patnas or something.

"If I'm up to it I'll be there by myself."

"I'll have to bring a couple of my ladies for you two," Dmitri laughed.

"Nah, you can bring a couple for him but I'm good," I replied.

"I might bring my lil' lady with me. I just met this fine ass bitch that I'm sure will put every chick up in there to shame. I gotta bring her so I can watch the niggas and the bitches salivate over her," Sy chuckled.

"Damn, shawty got it like that?" I had to laugh at that myself.

"Oh this bitch is bad. I promise you that homey," Sy said.

"Mmgh, I'm a have to see that for myself."

We continued to talk for the next hour and each time Dmitri and Sy got on the subject of my drug organization, I found a way to talk about something else. I wasn't about to let Sy take things over but I did decide to try him out and see if he was really as good as Dmitri said he was.

6: Rozalyn

"Mmmh!" I moaned.

I pushed his head deeper into the center of my sweet nectar and gently tilted my head back in pleasure. The only thing that could be heard in the room was my soft moans and the splashing noises Messiah made each time he licked and sucked.

"Shit!" I cried out.

It's been forever since I had a man touch me this way, hell touch me in anyway and the shit had me riding on the waves of ecstasy. I'd almost forgotten how good it felt to be pleased.

"Damn, oh damn! Shit Messiah!" I placed my hand over my mouth to stifle my moans. The boys were in their room asleep and that was the only reason I agreed to let Messiah in my home. We'd been dating since the day I had lunch with him a couple of weeks ago. I really liked him but I didn't know him well enough to be bringing him around my children.

"Wait...wait let me get the phone," I pushed Messiah's head back but he grabbed my waist tightly and wrapped my legs around his shoulders. "Ahh! Ohhh!"

My phone began to ring again, vibrating loudly against the dresser. I reached for it but it ended up falling to the floor, rolling a few feet away.

"I'm cumming! I'm--ahhh!" I began to shake violently as a release of my juices gushed out, covering Messiah's lips. He licked his lips as he stood to his feet and parted my legs wider than what they already were. I was so high off of this lustful feeling that I couldn't even move. I wanted to reach out and push Messiah away once he whipped out his long, thick piece of meat, but was frozen in place. It'd only been a couple of weeks and I wasn't so sure if giving it up so soon would be a good idea.

Would he continue to respect me? Treat me like a queen? Would he think I was a whore? I asked myself.

"Messiah, wait--I--" I protested.

"Come on mama," he leaned down and kissed my lips making it harder for me to say no.

Messiah reached in his pocket, pulled out a condom, and glided it over his dick. He lifted me up from the dresser and carried me over to the bed.

"Can I?" he asked lifting my shirt and taking my breast into his mouth.

"Can you what?" I asked dumbfounded.

"Can I put it in? I don't want you to regret it."

"Uh--I---yea," I gave in.

Once Messiah peeled his shirt away, I wrapped my arms around him and welcomed his touch. I could hear my phone steadily vibrating somewhere on the floor and wondered who was calling me. The thought quickly went out of my head when the tip of Messiah's rock hard dick penetrated my wetness.

BAM! BAM! BAM!

DING DONG! DING DONG!

"What the fuck?" Messiah rolled off of me onto his back and sighed. "You expecting somebody?"

"No, but that may be who's been calling me," I slid out of bed and rushed to my phone sitting on the floor.

The moment I picked it up it began to vibrate once again. Seeing Tamar's name light the caller ID up sent me into panic mode. Hesitantly, I answered.

"Hello," I said.

"Fuck you doing? Damn, Roz I done called you at least thirty damn times! Come open the fucking door before I kick this muthafucka' down!" Tamar yelled into my ear before hanging up.

"Oh shit. Messiah put your clothes on, you gotta go!" I frantically yelled.

I grabbed Messiah's shoes from the floor, his shirt, and raced in his direction.

"You serious right now?" Messiah asked.

"I'm very serious Messiah. My baby daddy is at the damn door. If he finds you in here shit won't be pretty," I explained.

"You still fuckin' the nigga?" Messiah asked getting upset.

"Messiah please it's not like that. I just got visitation rights with my kids and I'm not trying to fuck that up. Please---"

BAM! BAM! BAM!

My phone vibrated in my hand and sweat poured from my brow. I knew if Tamar found out I had a dude in here he would be livid. It wasn't even that I felt he would be jealous but having another man in the same house as his kids would likely get me and this fool killed. Not only that I didn't want him to go back to the courts and try to snatch what little rights I did have away from me again. Messiah took his sweet, precious time getting dressed and the fact that he did it with little urgency pissed me off.

"Nigga, hurry the fuck up!" I stared at him disgustedly.

He looked down at me after slowly putting his shirt on. The look on his face told me that he was mad but I didn't care one bit. The knocking at my door continued along with the vibrations from my cell phone.

"Tamar, I'm coming. I was in the shower, hold up," I lied once I answered the phone.

Messiah grabbed his keys from the dresser and left the room without breathing a word to me. I followed behind him and immediately grabbed his arm when he headed towards the front door.

"Messiah, back door please," I said with frustration clearly in my voice.

"Oh, I gotta go through the back door like I'm some bitch ass dog!" Messiah's voiced raised intently.

His accent was thicker than normal and I was for certain that Tamar heard him. I held my head down, shook my head, and regretted my decision to allow Messiah to come over. This would be the only and last damn time.

"Yea a'ight Ms. Lady you got that," Messiah said with a nod of his head.

Finally I got Messiah out of the house! I raced to the front door, took a few moments to catch my breath, and then opened the door. Tamar was standing in my drive-way, leaning up against Messiah's car.

"Tae!" I yelled at him.

He looked over at me but didn't move an inch. Messiah would be hitting that corner at any minute now and all hell was bound to break loose.

"Tae!" I called out again but he continued to post up on the damn car. "Look ain't nobody about to play with you. I'm about to go to bed."

"Who car is this?" he asked finally emerging away from the vehicle.

"The neighbors I guess. They park their car over here sometimes," I said and walked into the house.

I noticed Tamar look over his shoulder once more before coming inside the house. I stopped inside the foyer, folded my arms, and eyed Tae curiously. It was after midnight and the boys were asleep so what did he want.

"You let your neighbors park in your drive way all the time?" Tamar asked. He walked around me and began exploring my home without my permission.

"Tae, what do you want?" I asked.

"Yo, I know you don't have a nigga around my damn kids." Tamar continued surveying his surroundings, moving throughout the house with a limp.

"Ain't nobody here but me and the kids. What do you want?"

"Why the fuck you didn't answer the phone or the door then? You got somebody up in here Rozalyn?"

"I told you I was in the shower when you called! Don't be questioning me any damn way. Why the hell are you here?"

"Dude the one that kept you from coming to see me at the hospital? I know it's another dude in the picture so don't lie to me," Tamar had the nerve to say.

"Nobody but me kept me from coming to see you. I'm not your woman anymore and you ain't my responsibility. That's what your fiancé is for," I spat.

"That's not my fiancé. I didn't put that ring on her finger."

"Tamar, I don't really care. I'm just waiting on you to come to the damn counseling sessions so we can be done with each other."

"That's what you really want huh?"

"Yes, that's what I want," I nodded.

"I just came to pick my shorties up. I ain't seen them in a minute. Where they at?" Tamar asked. He kept his stare on me while rubbing the hairs of his goatee, seeming to be in deep thought.

"They're sleep. Why'd you come so late?"

"Cause I was handling business. You gonna go get them or not?" Tamar said.

I nodded my head and walked towards the boy's bedroom to wake them up. I don't know what was up with

Tamar's change in demeanor towards me. For the past year he's been hating me and doing everything in his power to make me suffer and now he all of a sudden care again. It was over and I mean that. Sick of the back and forth, one day he loves me and the next day he hates me and wants to kill me. I couldn't deal with that anymore.

"Ag--" I jumped when Tamar wrapped one hand around my mouth and an arm around my waist.

He leaned down and whispered in my ear, "You ever bring a nigga around my kids again you might as well run for your fuckin' life. I ain't stupid."

I nodded my head, placed my hand over my heart, and fought to catch my breath. That was the only and last time, I meant that.

7: Messiah

Miami is my fucking city. I own it. I claim it. It's mine. My first year in prison was smooth sailing; I still had control of the streets, my commissary stayed full, and everybody showed me major love and respect. All that started dwindling once I lost my connection. I started hearing shit about some young cat with milk still on his breath moving in and acting like he big time around this bitch; got my soldiers on the block for him, putting my paper in his pocket, and all that dumb shit. No lie, hearing that heated me to the core and was the only thing I thought about while doing the remainder of my sentence. Especially when the guards stopped giving me special treatment, the cats that once respected me gave me the side eye, and my fucking money stopped!

Payback is a bitch though. Tamar might not know he fucked up my life but he will find out soon enough. First, I'm a fuck his bitch, slowly fuck his world up, murder the nigga, and then continue to fuck his bitch. I heard he was a sucka ass squirl behind his baby mama and finding out they wasn't together anymore was like music to my ears.

I hated to come through and string Rozalyn along, she is too pretty, seemed like a good ass female, and not deserving of what I had in store for her. A beautiful chick that had her own was hard to come by where I'm from and as much as I hated to destroy her world; I just had to. The one thing I've learned since being in the game is to never show your opponents your weakest spot and unfortunately for Tamar; he showed his in Rozalyn.

"Sup mama. Thank you for meeting me," I kissed Rozalyn on the cheek and took a seat beside her.

"You're welcome," Rozalyn shifted in her seat uncomfortably.

"What you want me to sit on the other side?" I asked jokingly.

"I didn't say that. What's up? I didn't think I would hear from you again."

I exhaled, "I'm really just trying to figure out what's going on with us."

"What do you mean?"

"I thought you were feeling me, it's obvious that I'm into you. I just really thought we had some type of connection."

"I thought we did too. You really flipped out on me the other night."

"That's because you tasted so damn good to me and then your nigga came through and fucked it up," I said leaning and kissing her on her ear.

"We are not together anymore. I told you that already," Rozalyn sighed.

"Shit, I can't tell. The way you started to panicking when he came over. What's up with that?"

"He's crazy. I should've never had you over to my house. I know how that fool is and---I don't know. I just feel like I shouldn't even be trying to date anyone. I feel like I have to sneak around and I'm not trying to do that or put anyone else through that."

"Sneak around? What? You just gonna let him control your life? You already told me that he's engaged to someone else. Why the fuck would you need to sneak around?"

I couldn't believe this bitch was scared of this punk ass nigga. He obviously has done some fucked up things to her cause she looked like she would piss on herself just at the mention of his name. I don't give a damn what this coward did to her, I needed the bitch to get on board. Without her it would be impossible to take Tamar down the way I wanted and needed to. I could easily snatch his kids up and make a few threats but that would be too easy. I needed his chick and I needed her on my team.

"Look, I just want you to be happy. I want you to be happy with me," I leaned over and kissed Rozalyn on her neck. "I want you to be with me. Be my girl."

"I don't know. I don't wanna see anything happen to any-body else because of me. Tae will---"

"Tae ain't gonna do a muthafuckin' thing to me. I ain't scared of your bitch ass baby daddy. You must not know who the fuck you dealing with," I said getting angrier than I expected.

I was really sick of her sitting here acting like this clown was God and couldn't be touched. I grew up in a family full of killers from the men to the women. No man can put fear in my heart, especially not one that bleed red just like I do.

"Okay, let me out the booth. You are not the same person I met. I need to get back--" Rozalyn stood up but I grabbed her arm and pulled her back down.

"All I'm trying to say is I'm not some punk ass nigga. Your baby daddy don't scare me and as long as you and I are together he can't do shit to you. Believe that mama."

She bit down on her bottom lip as if she was contemplating what I just said. Damn, I guess I had to go back to playing a sweet heart ass nigga with her. I could see she wasn't feeling the real Messiah.

"Come here," I turned her face towards mine and kissed her lips. "You gonna come to my party tonight right?"

"Damn, that's tonight. You never told me where it was at," Rozalyn said seeming to relax.

I kissed her on her lips some more and then brought my hand under the table to rub between her thighs.

"When you gonna let me taste it again?" I asked nibbling on her ear.

"Stop, the waiter is coming finally," Rozalyn pushed my hand away.

The waiter came to the table to take our order and left us alone again. Once he was out of sight, I slid my hand between her thighs again, rubbing her pussy through the fabric of her clothing.

"Shit, Messiah stop," she moaned.

"You coming to my party or not?" I asked again.

"Ye--yea. Where is it?"

"Club called The Revolver," I answered watching her face twist up in confusion.

"Oh--I'm not old enough to get in there."

"You don't have to worry about that. I'll get you in there."

"Messiah, that's Tae's club. I don't think--"

I cut her off, "I don't give a fuck whose club it is. My money is paid and that's where I'm having my party."

"Well I'm not coming," Rozalyn sighed.

"You a trip," I shook my head.

***

I sat in my car outside The Revolver gripping the handle of my pistol, wanting so badly to just go up in that bitch blasting but thought better of it. I couldn't convince Rozalyn for nothing in the world to show up at my damn party tonight. I was beginning to think that maybe I needed to figure out another way to get at Tamar. He seemed to have Rozalyn under a tight hold making it hard for me to break through to her. I wasn't about to give up on her just yet though.

I shook my head, tossed the pistol underneath the seat, grabbed my shades, and got out of the car. I had to hide the fury in my eyes behind my shades knowing Tamar would be able to detect it.

"Hey Messiah!" a chick yelled out as I passed her up in the line.

I nodded my head at the bird and continued towards the VIP entrance. Both lines were long as hell but luckily I didn't have to wait. I walked straight up to the bouncer that guarded the door checking for names and ID.

"What's up big man, Messiah Christian," I told him my name and handed him my ID.

"Shit everybody is waiting for you. Come on in," he stepped to the side and handed me my ID back.

The club was all the way live. Bitches wearing their best fits, some most likely had the tag still tucked so they can return it and get their money back.

"Sy!" A few groupies yelled as I made my way to the VIP lounge.

Climbing the stairs to the VIP lounge. I could hear Tamar's voice clearly over the loud music. The nigga always wanted to be the center of attention. I finally convinced the muthafucka to come to my party a few days ago, only because I thought that Rozalyn would be coming. Now I wish the clown would leave. He's gonna make it hard for me to enjoy the celebration of finally being out the pen.

"Aye, what's up Sy?" Tamar's brother Taron greeted.

I looked around the VIP lounge and nodded my head in approval. I must be honest and say that The Revolver was competing with many of the top clubs in Miami and shit probably all over the world. A lot of money, time, and effort had gone in this spot and it only made my blood boil more. This was my money the nigga was spending. Mine!

"Sup, Ron? Y'all got it looking good up in here," I said giving Taron dap and making my way over to Dmitri. Fuck Tamar and that other clown, Kevin. "Dmitri, what's good?"

"Sy, my man. How is it going buddy? What do you think?" he asked.

I looked around VIP once again and then down to the main floors, they were sectioned off like three different clubs in one. Each were decorated differently with its own little theme. I assumed the music was different in each one as well 'cause they all had their own D.J. and the crowd danced a little differently in each one. The VIP sat on the second floor right above all three rooms, giving a clear view to each one. Surrounding the VIP were the upstairs levels to the main rooms downstairs. The shit was sick no doubt and I had to give Tamar and his bro credit for it all.

"Where your chick at?" Tamar asked as he tossed back a Corona. "I was waiting to see what this bitch was about."

"She might not make it, wasn't feeling too good this morning," I lied. I grabbed a Corona from the middle of the table and signaled for a waitress to come my way. This little beer wasn't going to do anything to subdue the hate I had for Tamar and it was too soon to reveal any of it now.

"Damn, that's too bad. I really thought I was about to be impressed tonight," Tamar said with a smirk. "It's cool, it's plenty bitches in the club. Pick one and we'll have one of the staff bring her up."

I laughed in my head. This nigga really thought that he was doing me a favor. If he only knew that it was baby mama that I planned to show up here with tonight, I bet he wouldn't be hollering about pick one then.

I shook my head. "Let me have a glass of crown black, straight."

The waitress looked around to see if anyone else wanted anything before walking away. Just as I leaned back in my seat for what I knew to be a long night, my phone began to vibrate deep within my pockets. Once I pulled it out and saw Rozalyn's name flash across the screen I almost hit the end button, but curiosity got the best of me.

"What's up?" I answered, yelling over the loud music.

"I'm here and my friend can't get in. Can you put his name on the list?"

"His?" I frowned.

"Yea, my friend Brian I told you about.

"Oh ok! I'll be down in a minute!" I shouted.

A slight grin entered my face knowing shit was about to be on and popping.

"Aye, now watch her shut the whole club down!" I said to Tamar and meant it literally. If my source was right about Tamar, the whole club was about to be shut down when Tamar saw me with Rozalyn.

8: Tamar

I need to talk to you!" Dmitri yelled in my ear.

I nodded and handed the blunt I was toking on to Kevin. I followed Dmitri out of the VIP lounge, through the club and up to my office.

"Who did the count Tuesday night?" Dmitri asked before we could even get in my office good.

"I did, why?" I asked sitting atop my desk.

"Everybody we supplied to has complained about the weight being short."

"Well that's impossible. I weighed every other bird as normal, counted each one of them three times."

"Some of the guys complained about not getting what they paid for, and what they did get wasn't weighing out right," Dmitri crossed his arms and looked at me defiantly. "You, me, and my father are the only ones that know about the shipment. I know I didn't touch it--"

"Wait a minute, what? I know the hell you ain't trying to accuse me of stealing my own dope! Fuck you getting at right now?"

"I don't know, you did complain about the profit my father and I were taking. I'm just--"

"You just about to write a check that ass can't cash muthafucka!" I jumped down off my desk and approached Dmitri.

Couldn't believe he had the nerve to sit here and try to accuse me of stealing from my damn self. Them my muthafuckin' birds! True enough I complained about the percentage that Dmitri and his pops was taking 'cause realistically the shit was unreal. I paid them for each brick and after I sold each one, I still gave them ten percent of what I made all together.

I didn't have to do that but being they gave me a playa rate I felt it was only right. Well that was before I started moving a hundred bricks or better a month. I'm paying all the foot soldiers, the security guards, police officers; everybody. They should be happy that I re-up on a consistent basis, same amount or more each time. Let's not even talk about the expansion process that's in the works. The re-up will only get bigger and better and they both needed to realize that.

"Tae, I've known you for years. Never once did I think you would skim from me and my pops," Dmitri threw at me.

"Dmitri, get the fuck outta my club!" I yelled.

"We'll see what you gonna do once that well runs dry."

"Nigga, last time I checked my paper was GOOD! Muthafuckas need me not the other way around. Fuck outta here man," I dismissed Dmitri.

Dmitri nodded his head and turned to leave my office "Fuckin' thief!"

"Yea, fuck you too nigga!"

Just as Dmitri went to open the door, Taron came through the door huffing and puffing like he'd ran the whole way up here. Dmitri harshly brushed passed him damn near knocking Taron over.

"Fuck is up with him?" Taron asked.

I shook it off and went around to the other side of my desk. Hearing that the weight was low had thrown me the hell off. This had never happened before and I know for sure, I didn't touch shit. I do the same routine each time, count it once it arrives, watch as it's loaded onto the truck, then count it once again when it's dropped off at the designated spot. Nothing was off when I left so the shit had me really confused. I can't believe that Dmitri would even insinuate that I was even responsible. For years I've worked with him and not once have we had this type of problem. No matter the case though, I can guarantee you that Dmitri would come calling me before I called him. If anybody didn't know, he knew that I was set for the rest of my damn life and the only reason I was still at this shit was so that my grandkid's kids; didn't have to work a day in their life if they didn't want to.

"Bro, did you hear me?" Taron asked snapping me from my thoughts.

"What?" I frowned.

"Look," Taron pointed to one of the surveillance cameras that taped the main floor of the club. I saw Sy's bitch ass, spotted Brian, and then--.

"Aye, I know that ain't Rozalyn!"

"Yo, I think that Rozalyn is the chick that fool been bragging about."

I leaned back in my seat and watched as Sy ran his hands down Rozalyn's ass, groped her, and then begin to kiss her. I was supposed to be over her but ever since the day I seen her at our court date, I realized I wasn't. I saw that very same, determined, smart, sexy Rozalyn I saw when we first met. The very thing that attracted me to her in the beginning was back and it made me not quite ready to let her go just yet.

Jealousy sparked up within me, along with the fire that Dmitri had already ignited. I knew it was a reason I didn't like this Sy cat, something about the look in his eyes told me he wasn't to be trusted.

"Hell no!" Taron yelled after seeing me grab my pistol.

"Ron, get out of my way!"

"Tae, chill out and besides Kari ass just showed up too!"

"Fuck Kari! I need to see what's going on with this situation here," I pointed at the screen.

"Bruh, I only told you so you wouldn't be surprised when you saw them together. We got a crowd full of people out there man. You need--"

I pushed Taron out the way before he could utter another word. Rozalyn knows damn well this fuckin' club is owned by me, so for her to show up for another man; only meant she was asking for trouble. The bitch was about to get what she was looking for.

I pushed through the crowd, animosity building with each step I took. Sy was holding onto Rozalyn's hand and whispering something in her ear. She spotted me coming her way and the look on her face instantly changed.

I assumed the crowd felt that something was about to happen, caused everyone began to look in our direction.

"What--fuck is up?" I asked.

"Tae, my man! I want you to meet my lady Roz---" Sy started but I cut him off.

"Your lady? This is my wife nigga! Your lady?" I repeated.

Rozalyn held her head down in shame, refusing to look up at me. I got closer to her and lifted her chin with the tips of my finger.

"Roz?" I questioned.

"Aye, my man she good. She's with me," Sy reached and tried to push my hand away when I turned and punched him square in his mouth. Blood instantly shot through the cracks of his teeth as he staggered backwards.

"Oh my God! Tae!" I heard Rozalyn scream.

Sy removed his shirt tossing it to the floor and walking back towards me. I shook my head before I hit him with two more quick ones to the jaw. He recovered and shot a couple in my direction that did nothing to me but further angered me. I moved towards him ready to put his ass down when security broke through the crowd and grabbed him up.

"Mr. Andrews, is everything okay?" one of the security guards asked.

"Get him the fuck outta here, and then clear this bitch out. We shutting down for tonight!" I yelled and looked over at Rozalyn. "Come here!"

"Tae, baby what's going on?"

Kari tugged at my arm, I snatched it away, and walked over towards Rozalyn. I jacked her up and pulled her through the crowd that was slowly dispersing towards the exit.

"Tamar!" Kari yelled.

I ignored Kari and continued up to my office, pulling Rozalyn along with me. Once we made it inside I pushed her onto the sofa and went to close the door. Kari appeared before I could shut it with a look of confusion on her face.

"Tamar, what the hell is going on?" Kari asked.

"Go home. I don't even know why you're here," I said becoming more and more frustrated.

"You invited me! What the hell do you mean? What is going on? I want some answers," she crossed her arms over her chest.

"Look, I need to talk to my wife! Take your ass home," I roared.

I noticed the tears that welled up in Kari's eyes but didn't care. I needed to see what the extent of this relationship was between Sy and Rozalyn. As much as I tried to let this girl go; I couldn't. Seeing her with this fool, allowing him to touch her, thinking that this was the nigga that was up in her house the other night; fucked my head up.

What the hell is going on? I thought to myself.

"Tamar?" Kari questioned. She looked at me then over at Rozalyn who sat quietly on the sofa.

"I'll be at the house in an hour. Just go," I slammed the door in her face and locked it.

For a few moments I paced back and forth wondering if I wanted to reopen a door that I thought I already closed. Did I wanna get back to the vulnerability that Rozalyn caused? Go back to being outta control with my attitude. Being in love again.

"What's up? What y'all got going on Roz?" I finally asked.

"We're just friends," she answered with her stare towards the floor.

"Just friends? I seen you kiss him, I seen you smiling in his face. It's more to it than that. Is this who you had around my kids ma?"

"He wasn't around the kids Tae, they were sleep. They never saw him."

"It don't matter if they saw him or not. You had this clown in the same house as my shorties! Do you even know him well enough to be bringing him to your house?"

"Yes, I know him. And why does it matter to you Tae? We have been split up for a damn year, hell over a year and you still acting like I belong to you! You're fucking engaged to somebody else and you wanna try and control who I date! Nigga fuck you!" Rozalyn stood up from the sofa and came in my direction.

"Fuck me?" I asked surprised that she said that.

"Yes fuck you! I wasn't going to show up here outta respect knowing that this was your damn spot but I said forget it. You're not about to tell me what I can and cannot do anymore. You're dating Kari and I'm going to be with Messiah, if you don't like it, oh well!"

"Nah, you---"

"Tae, it's over okay. You and I are done and there is no going back! Leave me the fuck alone!" Rozalyn turned to walk away.

I went after her, grabbed her, slammed her against the door and stared into her eyes. So damn beautiful to me. Every time I see her, she seemed to become more and more beautiful.

"Tell me you don't love me no more Rozalyn and I'll accept that. I'll show up to the counseling sessions and we can finish this divorce. Look me in my eyes and tell me that you done with me," I said.

"I'm--" she looked around then looked me into my eyes. "I'm done."

"So that's it, you don't love me no more?" I asked unable to accept what I was hearing.

"No, I don't. You've put me through hell and back again Tae. All the cheating, beating---"

"Don't act like I'm the only one that was cheating. Get your mind right and remember the shit you did to me too though!"

"If I fucked another man it's because of the way you treated me. You pushed me into the arms of Brandon!"

"So, I made you fuck my best friend Roz? I made you fuck him right before we got married, right after our fuckin' honeymoon---and I made you fuck him at Keylan's wake too? I made you do all that Rozalyn?"

Rozalyn's facial expression softened at the mention of her and Brandon having sex at Keylan's funeral. It didn't really take a genius to know that what I've been told was true. I wanted her to deny that shit, put some doubt in my head, but nothing; she looked at me with resentment and hatred, something that I never wanted to see from her.

"Tae, it doesn't matter what I did or what you have done. All I know is that I'm done with you. Let me go!" Rozalyn yelled.

"You think I'm a sit back and let you fuck with this nigga like I'm cool with it?" I yelled, voice peaking with more anger than I thought I had.

"Let me? You don't have a choice, now get the fuck back Tae!" Rozalyn shoved me, only slightly moving me away from her. "Tae, I'm serious I don't want anything to do with you. Go marry that bitch ass reporter of yours."

Rozalyn slid around me and exited my office without looking back, leaving me with a look of disgust and a horrible feeling that I knew would be hard to overcome.

9: Rozalyn

"Rozalyn!"

I looked up and noticed Tamar leaning against his truck a few feet away from my shop. I rolled my eyes, crossed my arms over my chest, and headed in his direction. After I showed up at the club last night and was greeted by Messiah all hell broke loose, but I didn't expect anything less. Tamar's territorial ass did exactly what I had expected him to do; act as if he still owned me not giving a damn that his fiancé was there or anybody else for that matter. The fool didn't want me but the minute he sees me with someone else he has the nerve to get jealous.

People can say that I was disrespectful for showing up at Tamar's club with another man all day but I didn't care. I was tired of caring about Tamar's feelings when all he did was treat me like shit. He kept my kids away from me, got engaged to someone else and has the nerve to tell me what I can and can't do with my life. No, I was sick of that, sick of him running all over me, treating me like I was less than a woman and taking advantage of my heart. True, I've done things to Tamar but only because he'd fucked my head up so bad that I couldn't tell what was right or wrong anymore. My sense of judgment had been completely altered by everything that had been going on around me. Tamar's cheating, him beating me, the rape, loss of my first child, my kidnapping times two, and so much more. *How can a person think straight after all that? How can I be loyal to someone who didn't care enough to be loyal to me after most of what happened to me was because of them?*

It took me a while to understand that I deserved better than what I'd been given over the past few years. I played the cards that life had dealt but I played them all wrong because I didn't know any better. Now that I knew a little better, no-- a lot better; Tamar was the furthest thing from my mind. Rekindling anything with him was out of the question and at this point all I wanted to do was see how I could get the divorced finalized without the counseling sessions. Tamar wasn't going to show up. He treated this shit like a game just as he did everything else.

"You don't have to look like that. I just wanna holla at you for a minute," Tamar said when I came closer to him.

"What's up? I got ten minutes before I need to open up," I said. I pulled my sunglasses from my face and stared into the eyes of the man that I once loved more than I loved myself.

"So you fucked him last night huh?"

"What? I know that's not why you're here!"

I turned to walk away but Tamar snatched me back and forced me to look at him. Anger was written all over his face but his eyes said something completely different. He was hurt. He was actually hurt by the fact that I'd found somebody else and wasn't giving in to his silly demands.

"I saw that nigga come to your house Rozalyn so don't even lie to me!"

"Lie to you about what? I don't have a reason to lie to you Tamar! Damn, I told you last night that you and I are over with! I'm not joking, playing around, or even lying to you! I wish you will show up at the counseling sessions so that we can get this whole thing over with! I don't even know why the fuck I married you! Damn, I was so fuckin' stupid," I huffed.

"Really? He got your head gone like that? Now you regret marrying me?" Tamar asked in disbelief.

"No one has my head gone! I can finally see clearly, and I see that you ain't shit! You never have been and never will be. You were a waste of my time and I honestly hate that I have three children by you. What the fuck was I thinking?"

"Aye, you better watch your fuckin' mouth---"

"Or what? You gonna hit me in it? Go ahead Tae! Punch me like you used to, choke me, slam me against the wall, slap me---what?"

"Damn, that nigga got you feeling out of sight, out of mind right now. You got a lil' courage now, huh?" Tamar laughed. He stepped closer to me, leaning downwards slightly. I didn't flinch one bit. There was nothing Tamar could do or say to me that would further hurt me than he already has. I gave him too much control before but now it was time for me to take it all back. He was going to respect me whether he wanted to or not.

"Nah, I ain't gonna hit you ma. I'm over that. I should've never laid my hands on you and for that I apologize--"

"I don't--"

"Nah, shut the fuck up and listen. I'm glad you found somebody and that you think you're happy---"

"No, I don't think--"

"Listen!" Tamar said through gritted teeth. "Like I said I'm glad you think you're happy. That's all that matters is that you're happy. But let me tell you this, once we sign them papers and finalize this shit just know that it's truly over between us. Don't ask me for shit, don't call me for shit unless it's concerning Marion, Zyir, and Zavier. When you find out that fool Sy ain't what you thought, definitely don't call me. I'll step back and let you do you, ma! You might think 'cause you got your own shit and all that, you know what you doing but you don't. Your ass ain't ever been able to see shit for what it really is. Never."

"Yea, whatever," I said walking away towards my shop.

"Whatever my ass! At least I ain't ever fooled you into believing I was something that I really wasn't. I've always been true to myself even when you didn't like it!"

I waved my hand in the air dismissing Tamar before unlocking the door to my shop. I didn't have time to go back and forth with him about my life. He could try to convince me all day long that Messiah wasn't this or wasn't that but I know for a fact that he treats me good; better than Tamar ever has. To me it was all that mattered.

****

Rain drops hit my window sounding like miniature golf balls as it fell. Several times I contemplated pulling over and parking until the rain let up but thought better of it. I was only a few minutes away from the house and couldn't wait to get inside and into some dry clothing. Because of the rain, work had been extremely slow and most of the day was spent gossiping about any and everything. Customers usually cancelled on days like these or just flat out didn't show. It was a strain on some of our pockets which meant we would have to work extra hard for the rest of the week to catch up. With me getting the boys this weekend, I didn't see how that was possible so there would most likely be no recovery for me.

Finally after what seemed like a long drive, I pulled my jeep into the driveway, hitting the button above me to raise the garage. Like always, I smiled as I pulled inside, feeling like my own home was welcoming me into its arms. Once I parked the car, turned it off and got out, I walked over to hit the switch that closed the garage. Turning the knob that led into the house, I pushed the door open but froze sensing something wasn't right. I reached into my purse, pulled out my cell phone, but was caught by surprise when a hand went over my face, and knocked my phone out of my hand.

I tried to scream but the force of the hand covering my mouth only muffled my cries and forced me into silence. I was pushed inside of my home, brought directly to my living room, and pushed onto the sofa. It was like they'd been here before, the way they moved through the place told me that they knew their way away around. My whole house was pitch black, making it hard to see who the shadow was that stood before me. The figure was tall with broad shoulders but I couldn't make out anything else.

"I should've just snapped your fucking neck," he said.

A huge lump formed in my throat as the sound of the voice echoed through my ears. I jumped up from the sofa, thinking of an escape plan in my head as he came closer and closer. I brought my hands up in defense before turning around and running towards the nearest phone in the house. He gave chase and my heart began to pound, overshadowing the thousands of thoughts that ran through my head.

Before I could grab the phone, he pulled me by my hair and yanked me into his arms.

"What you running for? I just wanna talk to you," he said forcing me to look into his green eyes that lit up the dark hallway.

"Talk--talk to me about what?" I asked trying to get over my fear. He'd never hurt me before but after all I'd done to him, that was liable to change.

"What the fuck Roz? After all I've done for you; you turn around and do all that shit to me," he said venom pouring from his mouth.

"I had to do what I had to Brandon. Shit got out of control and you killed Brittany and Keylan, you killed them!"

"None of that was supposed to happen and you know that. You turned me into the black sheep of the only family I ever had and then you turned your back on me!"

"It wasn't like that, you needed help and I just wanted to make sure you got it before you ended up dead."

I knew that this day would come. When I found out that Brandon was convicted of Brittany's murder due to temporary insanity and sent to a mental institution; I knew that he would come for me. I just didn't know when. The bad thing about being declared insane is that you can always click back into sanity and get the doctors to say that you're ready to be a part of society again. This is exactly what happened to Brandon, two years flat and here he is free as a bird; but obviously still out of his damned mind.

I looked up at him and noticed his eyes swell with tears. I never once thought Brandon was a monster which is why I always tried to prevent Tae from doing anything to him. He only needed help. His drinking problem had gotten out of control and he'd allowed our sexual encounters to be mistaken for love. I admit that I should've never crossed that line with him but Brandon knew better. He knew that I would never leave Tamar to be with him. Never. Those were thoughts of his; never once were they mine and not once did I ever convey the idea that it was possible to Brandon.

"Look, just let me see my damn kids. That's the only reason I came here," Brandon said as he loosened his grip around my hair.

"Your kids?" I asked as I turned to look at him.

He'd grown his hair out and it was slicked back into a tight ponytail. The scars that were once so clear across his face from the beating he took from Tamar were now barely noticeable.

"Hell yea my kids, where are they?"

"Have you lost your damn--B, I told you when I was pregnant with my twins that they wasn't yours."

"Yea, I'm not trying to hear that shit. I know for a fact that one of them has my eyes, so where are they?"

I stared into Brandon's green eyes and thought about Zyir, he'd had those eyes since he was born but I always hoped that one day they would change but they didn't. Zyir's eyes always stood out the same as Brandon's. In the darkness it was like a glow.

"They're not yours Brandon! You know that Tamar wouldn't keep them if they wasn't his," I said wondering if this was true or not. Tamar never mentioned having the kids tested but did he have to? That was mandatory for him and no matter what he always got a DNA test done.

Brandon chuckled as if I'd said something funny then began to walk around my house. I took that opportunity to get to a phone. Quickly I raced to where a cordless phone sat on the kitchen counter and unlocked it. I went to dial Tamar's number but froze wondering if I should be calling Messiah. Tamar wasn't my man anymore and although he knew the situation with Brandon, should I be calling him?

For a few seconds, I tossed the options around in my head and then finally called Tamar. Regardless if Tamar and I were no longer together, this was between us.

"Tamar!" I said breathlessly the moment he answered.

"What's wrong?" he asked and I could hear the concern in his voice.

"Brandon is here and--"

The cordless went flying out of my hand and crashed to the floor, disabling the battery. I pushed Brandon away and pulled the drawer open that held knives of different lengths and sizes. I grabbed the first one I could get my hands on and held it up in the small space between Brandon and I.

"Look Brandon, I don't want any trouble okay? You need to talk to Tae about this. He has custody of the boys and---"

"What? You let him take my muthafuckin' kids?" Brandon bellowed.

"Brandon, they are not yours! Why do you keep saying that they are yours? They're not!" I screamed.

Brandon stepped an inch in my direction, the knife shook in my hand as fear took over my body. I stepped back until I couldn't go any further and just stared at Brandon hoping that he would just leave.

"Fuck going on in here?"

I looked up and saw Messiah rush into the kitchen with a pistol in his hands.

"Oh God Messiah," I said relieved that he was here.

Brandon looked over at Messiah with a look of confusion written all over his face. The two stared each other down for a few moments before Brandon backed his way outta the kitchen.

"I'm a see my muthafuckin' kids whether you like it or not!" he said before he bolted.

"Who the hell is that Roz? What is going on?" Messiah asked snatching the knife out of my hand. "Told you, you need to get that damn garage door fixed. Shit is not closing all the way."

I stared at Messiah as I took deep breaths, trying to push circulation back to my heart. This was not something I really wanted Messiah to know about. What kind of woman would he think I was if I told him I fucked my husband's best friend. I had to think of a lie and quick.

10: Tamar

"Fuck you get out the car for?" I frowned at Kari.

"Because it's freaking storming out here. Why the hell couldn't you call Ron like always to handle her damn problems?" Kari asked.

"Look, if you got a problem with me coming to check on my damn wife go get your ass back in the car!"

I reached over and rung Rozalyn's doorbell and impatiently waited for her to answer. When she called me a little while ago, I could hear the distress in her voice and immediately dropped everything and came over. I wasn't positive but I could've sworn I heard her mention Brandon's name. I'd gotten word that he would be released soon and thought the muthafucka would've been smarter and stayed the fuck away.

"What's up?" Sy asked once he pulled the door open.

"Aye, where Rozalyn at?" I asked with a mean ass mug on my face.

"Chilling, what's up?"

"Chilling? Where the fuck she at yo? She just called me."

"Nigga, I said chilling. I'm here and she's good," Messiah sucked his teeth and went to close the door but I stuck my feet out to prevent it from shutting.

"Tamar, let's go! He said she's good," Kari chimed in.

I stared Sy down for a few moments before reaching into my waistline and pulling my pistol out. I'd already knocked this fool out in the damn club and he still wanted to try me, maybe after I showed his ass a little gunplay he would better understand not to fuck with me.

Sy chuckled, "You think you the only one that got pistols nigga?"

"Nah, I know for sure I ain't, but I know for damn sure I don't have no problem pulling the trigger," I said and cocked the hammer.

"Messiah, what---"

Rozalyn pulled the door open, and looked from my gun to me, to Kari, and then up at Messiah.

"What the hell is going on?" she asked.

"Aye, you better check this fool though for real. Shit you called my damn phone---"

"Yea, I did call your phone. I need to talk to you in private. I guess y'all can come in," Rozalyn rolled her eyes and stepped to the side so that we could enter. Messiah and I never took our eyes off of each other and I never released my grip around the handle of my gun.

I followed behind Rozalyn as she led me to the boy's room, closing the door behind us. She seemed to become frustrated to fidgety and nervous in a matter of seconds. Placing the safety on my gun, I placed it back where I got it from, and leaned against the wall waiting on Rozalyn to speak.

"What's up? What happened?" I asked.

"Did you have a DNA test done on Zyir and Zavier?"

"What?"

****

Hearing Rozalyn mention Brandon's visit and him claiming my twins made my skin crawl. I didn't sleep all night thinking about the things I wanted to do to Brandon once I saw him. The day he killed Keylan was always fresh on my mind. There was never a day that went by that I didn't think about Brandon and what he did. Brandon literally destroyed the only family I had left and the nigga had the nerve to show up like shit was cool. I definitely needed to see him and find out what's really good with him.

Even with Rozalyn saying she would never make the mistake of sleeping with him again; I didn't believe her. I knew the connection they had is one I would never understand. If he could talk her out of her panties at a funeral in a damn bathroom, then I could only imagine what else he could do.

I sat at a table in the back of a popular sports bar watching Brandon as he tossed back a beer. I see that it didn't take him any time to get back to his old ways. Fool didn't even have the decency to get his hair braided or a fresh fit and here he was already drinking.

I'd been sitting here for a couple of hours just watching and thinking; thinking if I wanted to kill him as soon as I got a chance or if I wanted to question him about everything. Once again when I threw the bathroom incident in Rozalyn's face and she didn't deny it or admit to it. I wanted to know if what Kari says she seen was true or not.

I waited at my table for a few more minutes only deciding to get up and approach him when I seen him order another beer. It didn't look like he would be leaving until he was put out, so I placed my plans of killing him on hold and decided to see what information I could get out of him.

"What's up?" I asked taking a seat on the stool next to Brandon.

He didn't look up at me at first, took a long sip from his beer, and then cut his eyes in my direction.

"Let me get a crown black, no ice," I ordered then brought my attention back to Brandon.

"What's good fam?" Brandon asked lowering his head towards his glass.

"Fam? Fuck outta here with that," I scoffed. "You tell me what's good. Heard you went to see Roz, what's up with that?"

Brandon shrugged his shoulders and took another sip of his beer. Dude looked bad as hell right now and I almost felt sorry for him. I know he had to be damn near broke if not broke. Lawyer's fees and restitution payments had to have hurt his damn pockets. But this is what happens when you fuck over family, especially when they were feeding you very well.

"Wanted to see my shorties."

"Your shorties, what you mean your shorties?"

"Yo, I seen pictures of the twins Tae. I know one of them has my eyes. No one in your family has green eyes; I know you got them tested. I'm gonna go to court and get my rights."

"B, you don't have no fucking rights! Them my muthafuckin' kids nigga! Look, I'm a tell you this shit one time only. Stay the fuck away from Rozalyn and stay the fuck away from my kids!" I yelled causing everyone to look in our direction.

"Did you get them tested Tae? That's all I want to know."

"You already know how I get down. Don't play me too close B, I promise you I got two bullets waiting on you. Try me," I stood up from my chair, tossed a twenty dollar bill on the bar, and proceeded to walk away.

Before I could leave, I had to know one thing so I went back to where Brandon sat, "That shit that happened at Keylan's wake--what Rozalyn said. Was it true?"

Brandon laughed, "You still on that? Damn fam, I bet it's been eating your mind up ever since then huh?"

"Answer my question," I said through gritted teeth.

"I never had a problem getting in her panties before, why would that day be any different?"

I snapped. My hand went to back of Brandon's head, where I slammed his face into the bar's countertop. Patrons of the Chili's began to scatter, trying to get away from the scene. I knew this wasn't the smartest thing to do being I had plans to murk him at a later date, but fuck it; hearing that shit pissed me off.

"Someone call the police!" I heard somebody yell out.

"Pussy ass nigga!" I spat.

I left Brandon with a broken and bloody nose and got the hell out of the restaurant. The one time that I chose to go based off of Rozalyn's word may be the one time she fucked me. Damn!

11: Rozalyn

A week later

I sat patiently on Brian's couch waiting for him to open the huge envelope that came to me today through FED-EX. I already knew what the contents of the package held but for some reason I was too scared to open it on my own. I don't know why I was so scared because I knew there was no way that Brandon was the father of my twins. Just because Zyir had those same green eyes meant nothing. Those eyes could've came from anywhere in my family or even Tamar's family. I didn't have anything to worry about; everything was going to be good.

"Just open it. Fuck it. I know what it says."

"Okay girl," Brian pulled his dreads from his face and tore into the package.

I leaned back on the couch, crossed my arms over my chest, and looked at Brian intensely as he pulled a white piece of paper out and looked over it. I noticed as his eyes squinted tightly and his mouth moved but nothing came out.

"What is it?" I asked sitting forward.

"Rozalyn it says---"

The ringing of my cell phone caused Brian to stop in the middle of his sentence. I looked down at my phone and answered when I saw Tamar's name pop up.

"Hel---"

"Where the fuck are you?" Tamar yelled before I could even get through my introduction. He didn't sound right at all. His voice cracked but it was filled with so much anger.

"I'm not at home Tae, what's---"

He cut me off again, "I know you ain't at home! Where the hell are you Roz? I need to see you now!"

"I'm at Brian's house. I can come to the house now."

"Hurry the fuck up before I come find your ass!"

Click!

"Shit!" I yelled shaking my head. I grabbed the paper out of Brian's hand and headed out the door.

***

I got out of my car feeling like I was going to fall flat on my face. My face was soaked with salty tears from all the crying I'd been doing and my eyes were red and puffy. Tamar sat on my porch putting on a thick blunt and stared towards the ground. Once I got closer to him I immediately broke out into more tears.

"Tamar, I am so, so sorry! I-I didn't mean for this to happen!" I cried frantically. My body literally shook knowing that all the failed attempts at trying to kill me was from luck and just God watching over me. I somehow knew that at this point nothing in this world could stop my death from happening.

"Open the door," Tamar finally looked up at me and I could see that he was more than high.

I walked over to the door, stuck in my key, and took very deep breaths before opening the door. Tamar followed behind me and slammed the door shut causing me to damn near jump out of my skin.

"Tell me this shit ain't true man! Tell me they fucked up somehow!" Tamar's voice peaked with anger.

I shook my head not understanding what was going on. I just knew there was no way possible that Tamar wasn't the father of my twins but evidence was saying differently. The results from the lab stated that the chances of Tamar being the father was at zero percent. I didn't get that. I was so confused, lost, and hurt.

"Them my muthafuckin' boys Rozalyn! I sit up and asked you when you were pregnant with them and you told me without a doubt they were mine! I fuckin' trusted you! How the fuck you gonna do this shit to me?"

"Tamar I didn't know! I thought---they were yours! It's not right; they had to have messed up on that test somehow. It just can't be."

Tamar took a toke off his blunt, blew the smoke out, and walked closer to me. I felt sick to my damn stomach as I tried to swallow the huge lump that formed in my throat. I looked up at Tamar with pity and sadness for what I had done. No matter what Tamar had ever done to me, he was a good father to those children and didn't deserve this.

"Them my muthafuckin' kids, do you hear me? Don't breathe a word of this shit to nobody! That nigga Brandon come around here again, send him my way. Not finna have them calling another man daddy! Fuck that! Those are my kids! Mine!"

Tears slid down Tamar's face and he tried to wipe them away but more fell. He crashed down onto my sofa, exhaled, and allowed his head to sink into the pillows. I stood in place, fidgeted with my hands, and silently thanked God. I could've taken advantage of this, at least gotten full custody of my twins, but I wouldn't do any of that. I was glad to hear Tamar say he was their father no matter what the paper said because I didn't want it any other way.

12: Messiah

2 months later

"Is that what you want?" I asked Rozalyn as she eyed a tennis bracelet.

She shrugged her shoulders and continued looking on at the expensive pieces of jewelry. She'd been really down over the past couple of months and although she told me nothing was wrong, I knew better. She'd taken some time away from her shop allowing Brian to run things in her absence so I knew something had to be up. I asked her several times if it had anything to do with the visit from that busta I caught her holding a knife to but was told that situation had been taken care of. I didn't know what was up but I was sick of seeing her down all the time and wanted to do something to put a smile on her face.

I honestly jumped into this shit expecting to play Rozalyn as part of the game I'd set up but recently things became deeper than that. We'd spent so much time together over the past few months that I couldn't lie and say that I didn't genuinely care for her. The feelings I'd developed were unexpected and came out of nowhere. Everything I had planned for her boy Tae had been tossed out the window because I didn't want to hurt Rozalyn in the process. I had to rethink everything I'd come up with to ensure that whatever I did, she wouldn't be affected in any way.

I could easily give up my plot to bring Tamar down since I'd already swindled his whole organization from underneath him but I wanted more. I wanted to watch him slowly crumble and then I wanted to kill him. Maybe if he hadn't embarrassed me in a crowded club, pulled a gun on me making me look like some kind of hoe then I would've stopped and been happy with the fact that I had my city back. Niggas like Tamar had to be put in their place because for some reason they felt like they couldn't be touched but I had to show him otherwise.

"Messiah did you hear me?" Rozalyn asked pulling me from my thoughts.

"I don't want anything let's go. I'm tired."

"You don't want anything? Why not?" I asked confused.

"Because this stuff is kinda expensive. I'm not about to let you spend that kinda money on me," Rozalyn smirked.

"If I got it, then why not let me spend it?" I questioned holding a thick knot of cash in her face.

"Cause that's a lot of money to spend on someone you've only known for a few months."

"What if I told you after only a few months that I was in love with you?" I said not believing the shit came out my mouth. It was real though, it's what I really felt and I wanted her to know that.

Rozalyn looked stunned. She broke her stare and began eyeing the same bracelet she'd kept going back to numerous times. I shook my head hoping I didn't put myself out there for her to just let me fall. The chemistry was there so I know I wasn't the only one feeling this way.

"Aye, let me get this piece right here," I told the employee.

A huge smile crossed her face as she walked over and pulled the bracelet out of the display and handed it over to Rozalyn. That bitch was icy and I knew for sure all them diamonds was about to add up.

"The price on that one is twelve-five hundred," the employee said with an arch of her eyebrow.

"The lady wants it so she must have it," I said. I peeled off one hundred and thirty hundred dollar bills and sat it on the counter.

Rozalyn looked up at me with softness in her eyes and mouthed to me the words "thank you." I nodded my head, leaned down to her, and kissed her on the lips.

"Anything for you," I said with sincerity.

After purchasing the bracelet, Rozalyn and I grabbed something to eat before I dropped her off at home. I had to meet with Dmitri and his father to go over the details of a shipment that was supposed to come in, in the next couple of days. This was the biggest shipment to date, the first time they'd ever trusted me with this much weight, the shipment that would guarantee my position on the throne. After this there would be no doubt about whom the King of Miami was and that coward Tamar would just be a distant memory in the drug game.

****

"Sy, how is it going my friend?" Dmitri's father Donald asked as I approached him and Dmitri.

"Everything is good sir, how are you doing?" I asked and had a seat across from him and Dmitri.

I looked around the backyard and nodded my head in approval. Donald's home was very immaculate, pricy, and decorated with class. His backyard had to be acres wide with a pool, Jacuzzi and more, making it seem that we were sitting at a fancy resort instead of his home. I smiled thinking this would be me in a few short years.

"Honestly Sy, I am not happy. I was just telling Dmitri that things are not good at all," Donald said snapping me out of fantasy world.

"Why is that sir? Have I done something wrong?" I asked pointing to my chest.

"Tamar---very, very smart young man. Very, very intelligent to be a black guy."

I sucked my teeth hearing Donald praise Tamar like he was some God. Nigga wasn't too smart if I was able to snatch his kingdom from underneath him with so little effort.

"I've cancelled the shipment that you were expecting and Dmitri will be talking to Tamar to see what we can work out with him," Donald eyed Dmitri incredulously leaving me to wonder what the hell happened in the last seventy-two hours since I'd spoken to Dmitri.

"Am I missing something? I thought that I was doing a good job moving the weight, sir," I said sitting forward in my chair staring at Donald in anticipation.

"Yes, for a rookie. You've successfully moved a total of twenty-three bricks in the past couple of months. That's chump change for me Sy. While you're moving so slowly, Tamar has successfully set up things in Dallas, Memphis and Louisiana! He still has control of Atlanta and is currently getting the right percentage of the clientele here in Miami!" Donald's voice peaked with anger as he counted off each city with his fingers. He took a sip of the dark liquor and slammed the glass on the table.

I sat back in my seat and tried my best to withhold my anger. That's why the fool hadn't been tripping about losing Donald as a connect. He'd somehow found a way around the shit and was still heavily eating with me not having so much as a clue.

"Sir, I---"

"I never wanted to get rid of Tamar! Definitely not for a muthafucka I've never dealt with before! No! I tried to listen to this dummy of a son that I have and believe that this man that's been working for me for years decided to steal from me! I've never, not once had a problem out of Tamar but yet I allowed this motherfucker here to convince me that a guy whose net worth is damn near fifty million dollars, stole a hundred thousand dollars from me. Does that make since to you Messiah? If you were worth fifty million dollars, would you risk your life over fucking toilet paper?"

Fifty million dollars? I thought to myself. *Fifty fuckin' million dollars.*

I could literally feel my blood boiling inside of my body. My temperature began to rise with the revelation of Tamar's worth. This fool had enough money to feed all the starving kids in Africa and still maintain a wealthy life. It pissed me off seeing that he saw more paper than the average dope boy would ever see in a lifetime, and yet he chose to be greedy and get more. My goal was to get at least ten million and quit but this fool was worth fifty fucking million and still grinding with no shame. Sucka ass nigga!

"I don't understand how Tamar is able to do anything. Do you not have control over who can move what in the city?" I asked dumbfounded.

Donald laughed, "That's not how I work Sy. I'm all about making money, not having wars and Tamar and the competition knows this. I don't do that petty beef shit that you blacks are so accustomed to doing."

"Tamar has hooked up with the Mexican Mob, a very dear friend of mine that I'd been competing with for years until Tamar came along. Once Tamar came in, I quickly shut everyone else down and no one else mattered but me. Now--- now those fuckin' Spanish spics are laughing at me and I don't like it," Donald groaned. "Fuckin' Spaniards will never let Tamar go. That's how they work, I have no idea how y'all are gonna get Tamar back but you better figure something out."

"I feel like if you just allow me to get my hands on this shipment then Tamar will not be needed."

"I would rather die a thousand horrible deaths before I allow you to embarrass me any further. Get the hell out of my face!" Donald waved his hand dismissively. "Get Tamar over here ASAP!"

I got up from my seat and headed towards the gate to leave. I felt like a sucker, like I'd been completely disrespected. Something my grandfather or my father would've never tolerated. Donald did not know my blood line, I would rather be homeless and without before I allow Tamar to be praised over me.

I jumped in my car, sped out of the driveway, and rushed to Rozalyn's spot. Whether she knew it or not, she was about to help me take this fool Tamar down. I wanted to get my hands on that fifty million, and I wanted to see him dead. Fuck seeing him suffer, he needed to be dealt with sooner rather than later.

13: Rozalyn

Since finding out my twins Zyir and Zavier didn't belong to Tamar, life has pretty much been hell for me. Nothing had changed between Tamar and the kids but I could see it in his eyes every time we crossed paths that he hated me. I think I was more affected by the results than anybody. As each day passed, the guilt of what I'd done has practically eaten me alive. It caused me to be depressed and I knew it was affecting my relationship with Messiah. Hearing him admit to me earlier today that he loved me completely shocked me. I knew for a fact that I didn't feel the same way because I didn't have the time to get to know him to even love him. We spent hours, days, weeks, and even months together but my mind had been so focused on that damn DNA test that I don't even remember half the time we spent together.

He treated me so good; so good that any girl that had him would feel blessed. I was that girl but with all that was going on I couldn't even allow myself to soak it all up. It had nothing to do with the money that he spent on me. Tamar did that but still didn't treat me as good as Messiah did.

The way he made love to me was something special, the way he talked to me, and listened as I talked, made me know that he was the man for me, but the timing was just so wrong. I couldn't fully return the love to him the way he needed with my mind being so jumbled with all this mess going on. He deserved much more than what I was giving to him.

Brandon had been blowing up my phone constantly asking to see the twins. I lied to him each time he called, not daring to tell him the truth, but it was like he knew otherwise. I could tell that he knew without a doubt that the twins were his. Even without seeing them in person, he must've felt a connection to them the way they say every parent feels for a child. Either way, I could never tell him the truth, Tamar would kill us both.

DING! DONG! DING! DONG!

"Shit, who is this?" I wondered as I went to the door.

I grabbed my purse and my jacket and then peeked out of the window before opening the door. It was Taron and he looked a little discombobulated.

"Hey, Ron, what's going on? You okay?" I asked a little concerned by his demeanor.

"Aye, Tae told me that you and him were about to meet up to talk about some shit. I raced over here to catch you before he left. I need to talk to you," Taron said sounding desperate.

"Okay--umm come in," I said.

I stepped out of the way for Taron to enter and then led him into my kitchen. I went into the refrigerator and grabbed one of Messiah's beers and offered it to Taron. He gladly accepted the beer and popped the top open, chugging down almost half of it in one setting.

"How is Journey?" I asked referring to his girlfriend.

"She a'ight---but that's not what I wanna talk about. Look at this shit man," Taron reached in his pocket and pulled out a crumbled up piece of paper and handed it to me. I straightened out the paper as best I could and noticed it was from a lab.

Wait. Did Tamar tell Taron about the twins not being his? I wondered to myself.

"Oh, did he tell you?" I asked.

"Did who tell me what? The damn lab told me."

"What? They gave you this? Did Tamar give you permission to get his results?"

"What the fuck is you talking about? His results for what? That's my shit!" Taron frowned and sipped on the remainder of his beer.

I looked at the paper closer and noticed that Zyir and Zavier's name was not listed but Keymani Daniels and the mother was listed as LaToya Daniels. I shook my head from side to side and eyed the paper with total disbelief. It said that there was no way possible that any other male could be the father of Keymani but Taron Andrews. I now knew what the conversation was regarding the day I overheard him at his mom's house.

"Oh my God Taron. What the hell?"

"One fuckin' time Roz! One time I was with her! I was drunk as hell and she came by the club while it was still under construction, we both drank and smoked and one thing led to another but I swear to you that it never happened again after that. Man I can't believe this shit! Keylan was my fuckin' dude and I know once Tamar finds out about this he will never talk to me again," Taron huffed and lowered his head.

"Oh wow. I don't know--I don't know what to say."

"She's threatening to call Journey and tell Tae! The bitch put me on child support even though I was giving her ass money every week for the past three months. She talking about she did it because I haven't been to see her!"

"What, do you not wanna see your child? Why haven't you seen her?"

"I don't know! I don't know! I'm just trying to figure out how to deal with this shit man. I got my man's girl pregnant, yo. I need you to tell Tae, tonight when you see him. Can you tell him for me?"

"What? Oh hell no!" I protested. There was no way I was going to tell Tamar shit! He'd already gotten news that Zyir and Zavier wasn't his and this fool wanted me to give more betraying ass news. Hell no! No! No! No!

"Come on Roz! There is no way I can tell him this shit but he gotta know because I need to see Keymani, I need to get to know my daughter before its too late. I'll deal with Journey but I need you to tell Tamar for me. Please?" Taron begged.

I looked down at the paper once more and knew that it would kill Tamar to hear this. Disloyalty was what he hated more than anything and as far as he knew Taron was the only one left with a little loyalty in him.

I nodded my head and agreed that I would mention the information I found out to Tae. I didn't know what Tamar wanted to see me about but I had to find a way to bring it up in our conversation.

***

The whole ride to meet with Tamar was like a blur. I had no idea what he wanted to see me about because he hasn't really spoken to me since we got the DNA results back. Out of the blue he text me and asked if I could meet with him and I agreed. I figured maybe he was going to tell me that he would finally take the divorce seriously and do what needs to be done to get it finalized. Since we didn't complete the counseling session within a timely manner, the case was closed out and now everything has to be done all over again. I honestly didn't know what Tamar's problem was. I no longer wanted to continue a relationship with him and I was confused on if he still wanted to be with me.

"Okay," I walked into the empty restaurant looking around cluelessly.

"Hello!" I called out unsure if I should turn around to leave.

The environment felt a little creepy and knowing how Tamar was, it felt like some kind of set up. He was so unpredictable with his moods and with me dating Messiah so publicly, and the twins not being his, I wouldn't put anything past him.

"Hello!" I yelled once again.

"Stop yelling," Tamar said into my ear causing me to damn near jump out of my skin.

"Fuck! You scared the shit outta of me! Don't do that!" I said hitting him in his chest.

Tamar laughed, "Where the boys?"

"Kevin is watching them. What's up? Where is everybody at?" I looked around again.

"It's just us. I wanted us to be able to talk without any ears. Come on," Tamar grabbed my hand and pulled me into the dining area of the restaurant.

In the middle of the room there was a single table lit up with candles, while soft music played in the background.

"No, no, no. What is this! Tamar let me go! Let me go!" I pulled away from him to leave when he wrapped his arms around my waist to stop me.

"Just sit down with me for a few minutes. Please?" Tamar begged.

"Candles and shit. You said we were gonna talk about some issues that's been bothering you. The hell is going on Tamar?"

"We gonna talk about all of that. Just sit down with me for a few minutes. That's all I ask. Just listen to everything I gotta say. I'll blow the candles out, turn the music off and all of that."

"Yea okay," I pulled away from his grasp, crossing my arms over my chest, and waited.

I knew he was up to something but I wasn't expecting this. All this romantic shit could only mean one thing. Tamar was trying to get me back under his hold and he knew the way to go about doing so. I was not about to let it effect me though, Messiah and I were going heavy right now and I decided after today that I would give him my full attention. He deserved that and more.

Once Tamar blew the candles out and cut the music, I walked over to the table and sat down but never let the mean mug leave my face.

Tamar joined me at the table staring at me with that sexy ass grin of his; the mischievous one he would wear when he was up to something. All you could see was the shine of his gold teeth but that smile held so much power.

"You don't have to look so mean. We just talking."

"Talk then Tae. I'm listening."

"What's up with you and this Sy dude? I see you still talking to him knowing that I prefer you didn't."

"Is this the issue that you needed to speak with me about?"

"Do you love him? Is it that deep? You going out to eat with him, to the movies and shit. Dude taking you shopping. What's up? What's going on?"

"What, are you following us? How do you know what we're doing? Shouldn't you be with your fiancé planning your damn wedding?"

Tamar sucked his teeth, "Aye, I never proposed to her. The bitch bought that ring while I was in the hospital after the explosion of my car. I'm not trying to marry her."

I turned my lip up and grabbed the bottle of champagne that sat on the table. I poured myself a glass and then slowly sipped.

"Real shit. She knows that I never got over you and the reason why we're not divorced yet is because I'm still holding on to what we had. I finally admitted that to her."

"What we had is exactly what it was. Tamar you have made my life a living hell since we split. You took our kids away and had them people take Shanya away. Zavier and Zyir barely know me and Shanya is living in the damn system."

"I didn't have them take Shanya away. I didn't know that they were gonna do that and as far as the boys go---I'm sorry. I should have never kept them from you. That was fucked up and---," Tamar sighed. "I know I can't take it back but honestly I'm sorry for that."

I didn't respond to his apology because I didn't understand it. Why now? Why did it take me fucking another man for him to apologize and see that he was wrong? If I'd known that was all it took, I would've done it months ago.

"Do you love him?" Tamar asked seeming as if the question took his breath away.

"Yes---I honestly do love Messiah. I'm happy with him and I want you to be happy for me," I answered knowing that it was only partially true. I was happy with Messiah but love, that's a powerful word.

Tamar scoffed, "Did you really just say that shit to me? Be happy for you?"

"Do I not deserve it; to be happy?"

"Yea, you deserve that and more but I wanna be the one to make you happy. Not sit back and watch another man do so."

"Do you even know how to make me happy Tae?" I asked laughing at the whole idea.

"Fuck is that supposed to mean?"

"It means that I don't think you know how to make yourself happy let alone anyone else. You so stuck on this perception that men of your caliber are too good to have feelings. You have a problem with women being in control and it irks you to see a chick making it without you, yet you holler about wanting an independent woman. You can't keep your hands to yourself, you're verbally abusive, manipulating, and can't keep your dick in your pants. What part of all that is supposed to make me happy? I can keep going if you're confused."

Tamar blew out air and leaned back in his chair. He then sat forward and was about to speak but a waiter approached our table carrying two plates of hot food.

"Can I get you anything else?" the waiter asked.

"Nah, we good for right now, 'preciate it," Tamar answered.

The waiter walked away and Tamar brought his stare to me. I could see that what I said to him hit him pretty hard.

"You never even gave us a chance at happiness from the very time you slept with my best friend," Tamar shot at me.

"Oh, here we go again," I huffed.

"Yea exactly cause you always wanna talk about what I did but never wanna talk about what you did. Damn, you fucked my dude at Keylan's wake. The kids that I've been thinking were mine all this time belong to that fuck nigga Brandon and you wanna throw salt my way like you haven't done shit!"

I rolled my eyes, pushed my chair away from the table and got up to leave. I know what I did was wrong but damn can he blame me? After all I went through with Tamar; I just felt the need to rebel. I loved him so much but all I got in return was bullshit. The twins being Brandon's wasn't planned and was never supposed to happen. If I could go back and change any of the mistakes I made, that would be one of the first; never sleeping with Brandon.

"Come here man," Tamar grabbed me and pulled me into his arms. "I still love you Rozalyn."

I closed my eyes and took a deep breath when Tamar stuck his tongue in my ear. His touch always did something to me which is why I tried to stay plenty feet away whenever I was in his presence.

"Tae, stop," I moaned.

Tamar ignored my protest, picked me up, and sat me on one of the nearby tables. I brought my foot up to push him back but he pushed his way through and stood between my legs. My pussy lips jumped out of excitement and my body shivered in fear.

"Love you Roz," Tamar leaned in to kiss my lips but I turned my head. He sucked on my neck and slid his hand up my dress, fiddling around until his finger was over my clit.

"Tae---come on now. I don't wanna do this."

"Look, I ain't going nowhere. After all this, I still wanna work it out with you. I want us to be a family again Roz."

"But I don't wanna do this....I don't—"

"You don't have to do anything. Just let me do me," Tamar said into my ear.

Before I knew it he was down on his knees with is head positioned between my thighs. I looked around the restaurant nervously, looked towards the entrance, and then down at Tamar. Part of me wanted to stop him but of course once his tongue dipped into my wetness there was no coming back from it. I leaned my head back, wrapped my legs around Tamar's head and braced myself for what I knew was an exciting orgasm to come.

"Damn," I moaned.

Excitedly I grinded my hips as Tamar lapped my pussy with his tongue, slurping me up like a dog left in heat. He sucked my clitoris, licked and pulled at it. My legs began to tremble violently as I gripped Tamar's head and pulled him in closer. He pushed my legs further back towards my head and dove in deeper, using his tongue like a drill, drilling inside of me, round and round, round and round. I could feel myself getting closer and closer to my peak and the slurping noises made me get that much closer.

"Ohhhhh!" I cried.

I pushed Tamar's head away but he gripped my waist tightly and continued pleasuring me until my juices squirted out all over the table, his face, and down my butt. I huffed and puffed to slow my heart down, stared at Tamar, and couldn't help but smile.

Shit! I thought. *He ain't never ate my pussy this damn good. I know he don't think he winning.*

Tamar bit his bottom lip as he stood to his feet, positioned his self between my legs, and leaned in for a kiss. This time I didn't turn my head, I took his lips into my mouth, sucked them, sucked my juices away, and closed my eyes when I felt his hardness enter me with such sensitivity.

"I need you back home," Tamar said before kissing all over my neck and chest.

"Tae, can you stop!" I said pushing him back. "Stop, stop! I don't wanna do this and I don't appreciate you bringing me here without telling me what's going on!"

I pushed Tamar as far back as I could, jumped off the table, and went for my purse. Feeling him inside of me almost made me forget how good he felt, how much of a perfect fit he was for me. I didn't need anything getting in the way of me making sound decisions. I'd been doing so well and the last thing I needed was for this nigga to get in my head again and have me all fucked up.

"Rozalyn come here, you trippin'!" Tamar yelled and reached out to grab me but I backed away and tried to move around him.

"No Tae, stay away from me. Don't call me if it's not concerning our boys. Just leave me alone! Please?" I begged.

"Damn, do I gotta get on my knees and beg you? What the fuck?"

"No, I don't want you to beg me Tamar—I just want you to leave me alone and let me be. This is what's best for us."

"How the hell you gonna say what's best for us? I've been fucked up since we parted ways, this shit can't be what's best. Come here and let's talk about this."

"I don't wanna talk about it Tae, I don't," I wiped my face with the back of my hand, aiming to get rid of tears that were beginning to fall.

I just felt like Tamar set me up knowing that this was all it would take to get me back where he wanted me to be. I just couldn't go back, back to when I was so weak and unable to think for my damn self. He didn't understand what it meant to love someone or to even allow someone to show him love. I'm not fully blaming Tamar for all the wrong that I've done to him but I did partially blame him. His ways had rubbed off on me, Brandon, and everyone else around him. Someone that possessed as much power as Tamar did was automatically put into a position of being a leader, a leader that had no idea on how to lead others. He led recklessly and because of that those around him followed recklessly. If he'd loved strong and without fault, those around him would've done the same.

One thing I've learned since being away from Tamar is to lead my own life, think for myself, and most importantly do for myself. Tamar was a huge weakness for me and since I knew that, it was best for me to stay as far away from him as possible.

"There's nothing to talk about. It's too late," I sighed. I placed the crumbled up DNA results that Taron gave to me earlier in Tamar's hand and walked towards the door.

"Don't say it's too late. After all we've been through, you gonna say it's too late? Rozalyn, don't walk away from me! I'm begging you! Please?"

"I'm sorry Tae. I just can't," I unlocked the door to the restaurant and left without so much as looking over my shoulder. Water flooded my eyes and threatened to fall but I held them back, held my head up high, and made my way to my car. I knew that this decision was the best decision I'd ever made in my entire life.

14: Messiah

Tick-tock. Tick-tock.

I could literally hear the sounds of time ticking away as I sat in my car waiting and watching for Rozalyn to return to her home. The minute I left Donald's crib, I came straight to Rozalyn's house. I noticed that she wasn't home but once again didn't check to make sure her garage door closed all the way. I decided to sneak in while she was gone and roam through some paperwork she had lying around, fishing around for any financial information she may have had lying around. Once I didn't come up on any relevant and useful information, I came back to my car and waited.

Sitting on the darkened street, I surveyed the clock for each minute that it changed. My stare never left the clock, watching, and wondering how long before I got tired of sitting here. Hours had gone by, the light had turned into night, and the innocent were in their beds sleeping. Only fools, drug dealers, and murderers were out and about at a time like this. Rozalyn wasn't a damn murderer; her baby daddy was the drug dealer, so a fool she had to be. A fool I must've been as well to actually sit here waiting and watching for her to return.

My mind kept going back to Donald's statement about Tamar being worth fifty million dollars and I couldn't help but wonder if Rozalyn had any of that money. Just looking at her home, I knew that it was impossible for her to be able to afford it and drive a brand new car working at a beauty shop. She barely even did hair and most of the time, sat around telling other muthafuckas what to do. She hadn't even worked a day in the past couple of months and not once did she ever ask me for a dime to help out on a bill.

That nigga had to be giving her money or gave her money that she had stashed away. I wasn't trying to steal anything from her but I needed to know if she was aware of Tamar's worth and if so, what info did she have that could be beneficial to me.

I'd been slaving my ass off for Donald and Dmitri these past few months and had only made a couple hundred thousand dollars. In the beginning, I had only wanted to make Tamar suffer and then kill him but now things had changed. He'd taken so much from me while I was locked up and it was only right that I took it back. That money that he was sitting on was partially mine. He didn't get my permission to set up shop here in Miami or use my soldiers to sell his work, and I damn sure didn't hand him my crown. Everything I had before I went down Tamar had snatched from me and it was only right that I snatched it back.

My eyes went over to my window after hearing a light tapping sound. Rozalyn stood on the outside of my car, her hair was a mess, her clothes seemed to be disheveled and out of place, and her eyes were glossy and low.

"You gonna sit out here all night?" she asked.

I sat my seat forward, glanced at the digital clock once again, and shook my head. I felt like some square ass nigga whose bitch took advantage of him 'cause she knew she could get away with it. I rolled the window down, gave Rozalyn the once over and frowned. A strong aroma of another nigga's cologne seeped from her pores letting me know what time it was. I just really hoped that she wasn't out creeping with that fuck nigga Tamar, which would only piss me off even further and cause me to end up doing some shit to this girl that I didn't wanna do.

I raised the window back up without even saying anything to Rozalyn and had to catch my breath and calm down before things got crazy between the two of us. I needed her to complete my task and honestly I didn't want to lose her to that chump. After a few moments, I got out of the car and went into Rozalyn's home, I could hear the water running from the back bedroom and laughed at how quickly she'd gone to take a shower. I made my way to her bedroom, looked around until I spotted her cell phone sitting on the nightstand. Checking over my shoulder to ensure that she wasn't coming, I walked over to the nightstand and retrieved her phone, pressing the button at the bottom that lit the screen up. Text message after text message had came from Tamar's phone and a few missed calls from him as well.

"What are you doing?" Rozalyn walked over to me and jerked the phone out of my grasp.

"Is that who you were with tonight, while you had me waiting five or six hours for your ass to come home?" I asked.

"I told you earlier when I talked to you on the phone that I had a meeting with someone; afterwards I went out for some drinks with Brian."

"Yea, and that's why you coming up in here smelling like that nigga's cologne!"

"Look, I don't know what you trying to accuse me of but Tae is bringing the kids over early in the morning and I need to get some sleep before they get here. I'm tired," Rozalyn walked away.

"Aye, come here. I'm not done talking to you!" I rushed after her, grabbed her by her arm but she jerked away, tripped and fell into the dresser, hitting her head on the corner of it. "Oh shit!"

I brought my hands up to my head, shook my head dizzily as shock took over my body. Looking down at Rozalyn, I couldn't tell if she was dead or alive. Blood was squirting from a big gash in the center of her forehead, her eyes were closed, and she didn't seem to be breathing. I took a seat on the bed and tried to figure out what I was going to do next. If she was dead, there was no doubt the blame would be put on me, sending my ass right back upstate behind them damn bars. There was no way I was going to allow that shit to happen. All I did was grab her and she was the one that pulled away and tripped over her own damn feet.

"Fuck! What am I supposed to do?" I wondered aloud.

Just when I thought I was more fucked than the first time I went to jail, I noticed Rozalyn's leg move around. I took a deep breath, let it out, and ran to her side.

   ***

"Careful, careful!" I said as I helped Rozalyn out of the car.

I sat at the hospital with Rozalyn for hours praying and happy that she was okay. I was questioned so many times by various hospital staff that I started to believe the lie I was telling myself. There was no way I could tell them the truth about what happened regardless if it was an accident or not. I knew if I admitted that I grabbed her they would take it for what it wasn't and lock my ass away.

After they bandaged her wound and ran a few tests on her, they discharged her with directions to stay off her feet and get as much rest as possible. I drove her home with few words said between us. I didn't know if she remembered what happened being she didn't bring it up.

"What the fuck happened?" Tamar asked.

"I'm okay---hey boys," Rozalyn said wearily.

Her speech slurred from the pain medication that they'd given her at the hospital. She looked like she'd just gotten out of a massive fight. A huge knot had formed around the gash, blood had dripped onto all of her clothing, and her hair was all over her head.

"I got it from here playboy. Kick rocks nigga." Tamar said a little too eagerly.

I nodded my head and went back to my car knowing the nigga was just putting on a show 'cause his shorties were around. If he really was talking about doing something he would've done it already. Fools like him only ran their mouth because they had one and didn't know what else to do with it.

I'm sure that muthafucka wouldn't know how to bust a grape. He was a fuckin' rich boy living in the damn suburbs, driving around in fancy cars, and blowing money like there was no tomorrow. Cowards like him didn't scare me one bit. I'm sure he didn't know the first part about getting gutter, as a matter of fact, I'm about to show him how gutter I can get.

I got in my car, slammed the door shut, and quickly cranked it up. I watched on in anger as Tamar opened the door for Rozalyn, swept her off her feet and carried her into the house. The fool was trying to pull out all stops to get shorty back and I wasn't about to let this shit happen too. He'd already taken everything else from me, my money, my status, and now the first chick that I had cared about since before getting locked up. This shit was getting more and more personal by the minute.

I backed out of the driveway, drove about five or six houses down, and parked the car before hopping back out. I looked around to see if anyone was looking and when I didn't see anyone, I pulled out my pocket knife, and headed back towards Rozalyn's house.

"This shit better work this time," I said with a smile. "Lights out bitch!"

15: Tamar

"Did he hit you Rozalyn? That's what I wanna know. You ain't making any sense to me right now," I yelled surveying the damage to Rozalyn's forehead.

"No, I told you he didn't hit me. I tripped and hit the dresser. He never put his hands on me so calm down."

"You sure? Don't lie to me and don't try to protect him!"

"I'm not lying Tae, he never put his hands on me. Can you please stop yelling? You making my head hurt worse," Rozalyn said as she propped a pillow up on the couch.

"Yea, a'ight. I'm about to go take them to my moms and I'm a be right back. Do you need anything before I leave?"

"No, I'm just gonna lay here and take a nap. I'm really tired right now."

"A'ight, I'll be right back."

"Give me a kiss Marion before you go. Mama will see you later, okay?"

Tamarion jumped up on the couch, gave Rozalyn a kiss on her lips, and then gave her a hug. The look on his face told me that he knew something wasn't right with his moms. Instead of letting her go, he continued hugging her until the twins came over and got in his way. They showered her with hugs and kisses, only pulling away when I made them. This was the reason I hated my family had been split apart in the way that it has. My boys needed their mom around and not some wannabe that Kari was being. She didn't know the first thing about being a mother and acted like one whenever she felt I was watching. Even if Rozalyn chose to never get back with me, I was about to get rid of Kari's leaching ass real quick. I finally admitted to her that I was the reason for my divorce being held up hoping that would make her move around without me forcing her hand but it only made shit worse. She was needier than she'd ever been and the shit was bugging the hell out of me. I looked forward to my days of being out on the road handling business or just whenever I was out of the house just so I could be away from her.

I leaned over and kissed Rozalyn on the cheek, watching as she drifted off into sleep. I grabbed her keys from the coffee table, and motioned for the boys to follow behind me.

After putting the boys into the car, I cranked the car up and started to back out of the driveway. I slammed on the brakes after hearing a pounding noise against my back window. I reached for my .22 that I had tucked away in a hidden compartment, cocked it, and rolled my window down.

"Aye bro let me holla at you for a minute!" Sy yelled as he approached.

"Nah, but you can holla at this .22 nigga! What the fuck you trying to do?" I asked making my pistol visible.

"I thought you were leaving the kids with Rozalyn. What's up? What happened?"

"Aye, hell is wrong with you? Fuck you questioning me about my kids for nigga?" I jerked my seatbelt off, placed the truck in park, and jumped out.

"I'm just saying. That's the reason Roz rushed from the hospital 'cause she knew you was coming through to drop the kids off."

"Say I'm a give you a fair warning. Stay the fuck away from Rozalyn and stay further away from my damn shorties! Get that in your head!" I pointed the hammer in his direction and watched as he backed away. I knew this fool was a damn lunatic! Only if I could get Rozalyn's ass to see this shit; see that this dude was out of his damn mind, but her ass never saw shit for what it really was. Sy was supposed to be gone a long time ago but yet he popping up behind my truck asking me about my damn kids like he was up to something. That didn't sit well with me and because of it; this was the last time they were coming around here no matter what Rozalyn had to say. If she wanted to see them again, then she would just have to bring her ass to the house.

Perfect for me. I thought as I got back in my truck and this time backed out, speeding down the block.

"Aye!" I answered the phone once I saw Dmitri's name pop up.

"Tamar, we need to talk," Dmitri said.

"Last time you said that to me, you accused me of stealing. I really don't have anything to talk to you about," I said as I came to a red light.

"Listen, about that, I just want to apologize to you. My dad had really been on my ass and the shit was stressing me out. I took it out on you and I shouldn't have. Let's meet up so we can talk about some things that I think will be very beneficial to you."

I laughed, "Talk to Sy, Dmitri. I'm sure you're aware that I've made a deal with the Mexicans. That's where my loyalty lies now and you know how I am about loyalty."

"I understand that. I think we can work something out with Rico and his dad if you can just hear me out. You know you're like my son--"

"I used to believe that I was like your son Dmitri. I had a lot of respect for you up until that very day but honestly I just can't fuck with you or your pops on that level anymore," I said and hung up the phone.

I tossed the phone to the passenger seat, turned the volume up on the stereo, and smashed the gas as I entered the freeway. I knew that it wouldn't be long before Dmitri or his pops came calling me. It had only been a few months since I hooked up with the same cats that had been nearly taken down along with me and Dmitri almost a couple of years back. The same dudes that I had to hide my family in Puerto Rico for in fear that they would come after them thinking that I had set them up when in actuality it was that fool Money that I had brought on my team and trusted with my life. I was able to get the situation resolved back then with no blood really lost and no harm done to our business relationship. Rico's father Ricardo had been watching Donald make millions and millions of dollars off of me and was eager to get me on their team so that he could take over and finally get his share of the big ass pie we were all trying to eat off of.

I don't know what Dmitri was thinking of when he came at me the way that he did. He should've known that I was the only reason that he and his father were able to see more money than they ever had. I established the relationship with the streets, got my hands dirty while they sat back and pretty much played the banker. My customers didn't know Dmitri, didn't know Donald, and they damn sure didn't know Sy. There was no way if they were smart that they would cop from some muthafuckas that they had never seen in their lives. Because I had been dealing with most of these people for years, they would follow me wherever I went, even into retirement. You had to be smart in this game if you ever wanted to make it, and getting rid of me was the dumbest thing one could do.

"Turn it up daddy!"

I glanced over my shoulder to see all three boys bobbing their heads to "Bag of Money" by Rick Ross. I chuckled to myself then pumped the volume up, bringing in a little bass from the dynamic sound system that was installed. I looked down at the dashboard and noticed that I was going eighty-five miles an hour; a little too fast being I had the kids in the car. I slightly pressed down on the brakes but the peddle went all the way down to the floor seeming as if it didn't have any pressure behind it. Suddenly my brake lights came on, a loud beeping noise mixed with the sound system, and panic began to set in. I glanced back at my boys once more and noticed that they were still entranced by the song and was unaware of what was going on. I just had to get the car to slow down on its own and everything would be cool. This was a brand new fucking truck that I just purchased a few months ago after my other truck was blown the hell up so I didn't understand why the brakes would be failing.

The speedometer slowly winded down as it reached sixty and then fifty, my heart rate slowed a little thinking a few more miles down the stretch of the freeway and it would slow down even more. I nodded my head along with the kids to keep them distracted and their minds off of what was going on. The last thing I needed for them to do was panic and start hollering and screaming.

I put my signal on, got over in the right lane, and wondered if I should get off at the next exit or wait until the one after. Just as I passed up the next exit a car cut in front of me, I slammed the brakes out of reflexes, the car jerked to the right, to the left, and then back to the right again. The speedometer suddenly read seventy miles per hour as I lost control of the car and veered off into the exit I hadn't planned on taking. Things suddenly went black as the front end of the car slammed into a hard brick wall.

BLAM!

16: Rozalyn

BAM! BAM! BAM!
DING DONG! DING DONG!

I was laying on my couch in a deep sleep, slob dripping down the side of my mouth, confused for a moment about where the hell I was when I heard someone going crazy on my door. I figured it was Tamar because he said that he would be back after he dropped the boys off with his mom. I slowly got up from the couch, brought my hand up to my head, and flinched at the pain of the wound and knot that had formed on my forehead. I couldn't believe that I tripped the way I did and damn near killed myself by running into the dresser. I know that if Messiah wouldn't have grabbed a hold of me the way that he did then it probably wouldn't have happened but I didn't blame him for it knowing that it was an accident.

"Who is it?" I asked and pulled the door open without waiting for a response.

Standing in my doorway was Taron and my brother Kevin, whom I hadn't seen in a couple of months. They both looked concerned, angered, and like they would snap at any moment. I looked back and forth between each of their faces and waited on one of them to say something to at least let me know what was going on.

"Dude got you that occupied that you can't answer your damn phone?" Taron asked with a menacing glare.

"Taron, I'm so sick of you coming over here like you my – "

"Roz, Tamar and the kids were in an accident. They are all doing okay except for Zavier. He's in critical condition."

My brother Kevin reached out to grab me before I fell to the floor. I had suddenly became light-headed, my body became fluctuated with heat, and several flash backs began to shoot through my head. Memories of my brother Zavier being killed by Tamar's brother Taron rushed through my head. The bullet hole that sat in the center of his head, the blood that leaked out onto the floor and the fact that he was killed due to no fault of his own ran through my head hitting me hard with no mercy. I wondered if I'd jinxed my child in some kind of strange way by naming him after my deceased brother. I wanted his memory to live on through my child being we would never get a chance to see his. His girlfriend Jazlene found out that she was pregnant shortly after he'd been killed but unfortunately no one has been able to contact her. My daddy Korey has tried numerous times to get in contact with her along with me and Kevin but we've had no such luck. I've always wondered what my niece or nephew looked like, what they sounded like, and if they were doing okay. One day I would put more of an effort into finding Jazlene the same as I would work on getting Shanya back and out of the system.

"Look we need to get you to the hospital. Tamar just called and said they need blood for Zavier. Let's go!" Taron said.

Lord please don't let me lose another child. Lose this Zavier too. I thought to myself as I followed Taron and my brother Kevin out of the house.

    ***

I rushed through the automatic double doors of the hospital's emergency room, and scanned the room for anyone that I knew. I didn't see Tamar, Tamarion or Zyir so I raced over to the nurse's desk to see if they could point me in the right direction. The whole ride over here was a slur of different images, everything that Kevin and Taron discussed in the car sounded like gibberish to me. The only thing that kept running through my head was that my baby wasn't doing so well. The thought of losing him just when I was getting to know him again felt so surreal since I lost my brother Zavier just when I was getting to know him. My son Zavier had been without me for a year and now I had to face the fact that he could die and that hurt more than anything in this world.

    "Excuse me," I said to the lady behind the big round desk.

    "Yes?" she looked up at me with a huge smile that quickly changed to a look of concern.

    "Umm, my husband and my three sons were brought in here after an accident. Can you tell me where they are?"

    "What's the names?"

    "Tamar Andrews, Tamarion, Zyir, and Zavier Andrews."

"Okay yes, if you would just go through here and take a left. They are in room T310."

I nodded my head and signaled for Kevin and Taron to follow me. We went through the door, made a left, and found room T310 just as we were instructed to do. Tamarion and Zyir were both lying in their own separate hospital beds with Tamar sitting between the two of them. Tamar got up from his seat, walked past me and over to Taron. He raised his hand and punched Taron so hard in the face that he ended up stumbling backwards and hitting a table full of instruments before he ended up hitting the floor. I moved closer to Tamarion and Zyir not knowing what the hell was going on.

Did Taron have something to do with the accident? I thought to myself.

"I'm just now reading that balled up piece of paper that Rozalyn gave me last night. I can't believe you bruh! You went behind Key back and got this bitch pregnant! I can expect some shit like this from this fool here," Tamar said as he pointed at my brother Kevin, "But not from your ass. This shit is fucked up and you know it. Even more fucked up that you had to get Rozalyn to tell me instead of you coming to me like a man."

"What the hell is going on?" Kevin asked as he moved closer to me and the kids.

"Toya's baby Keymani is mine," Taron said as he got up from the floor and wiped blood from his lip.

"What? Fuck you mean?" Kevin asked with a huge frown on his face.

"It happened one time, we were both drunk and that was that. It never happened again after that. I ain't know she was gonna get pregnant, I never once even thought that baby could be mine after that one fucking time. Damn!" Taron shook his head and paced the space of the small hospital floor.

"Okay enough of all that. I need to know what's going on with my boys and where is Zavier? Ya'll can have this discussion later," I said intervening.

There was really nothing that could be done about Taron being the father to LaToya's baby just like there was nothing that could be done about Brandon being the father of mines. What's done is done and there was no going back and changing any of it. We all had to accept our faults and move the hell on. Right now my main concern was my children and not this who was fucking who bullshit.

"Kevin!" I yelled.

"I can't believe you man!" Kevin yelled. He walked out the room, bumping into Taron as he left. I knew the only reason he was pissed was because he and Toya were still sleeping around every chance they got. She was living over in Keylan's mansion, spending up whatever money that he left, and having the time of her life. We really didn't speak much because I felt as if she didn't deserve everything she got after Keylan's death. They weren't together when he died, he'd moved on with Starr, and I felt that if anybody should've gotten anything it should've been Starr and not Latoya.

"Look, where is my son? We don't have time for all this other bullshit. Where is Zavier?" I asked again.

"He needs blood. I can't give him blood because of course I'm not his fucking father! You need to take your ass down there to that nurse's station and see if you are a match," Tamar said. He wrapped a towel around his arm, pulled on it, and went back to the chair he was sitting in before.

I caught the confused look that Taron gave the both of us but I wasn't about to speak on it. I kissed both Tamarion and Zyir on the forehead and then left the room to see if I would be a match to give Zavier some blood. I didn't know his condition but I hoped that someone could let me know something quick.

17: Messiah

"Look, there is nothing that I can do about it okay! My dad doesn't want to deal with you anymore, he asked that you no longer call him or show up to his house; just act like you never even met him!" Dmitri yelled as he slammed an empty glass down.

"How the hell — what the hell does he mean? How am I supposed to get money if I don't have access to any work? That nigga Tae was stealing from ya'll and you wanna sit up here and put this shit on me like it was my fault!" I said

"Messiah, I find it funny that we've never had these kind of problems until you came around. A whole brick comes up missing after Tamar is gone, money is not right, client's weight is off! I don't know, I thought that you were somebody I could trust and you made me look like a fucking fool. I should've gotten rid of your ass when Tamar told me to."

"Oh really? You let that fuck nigga tell you what to do huh? I'm sure he had something to do with ya'll getting rid of me now. How am I supposed to live Dmitri? Let's not forget that my grandfather made your dad plenty of money back in the day. I deserve the right to be able to do the same."

"You keep talking about your grandfather doing this and that but what have you done? You were just some nickel and dime hustla living through your damn grandfather! I boosted you up and you fucked me over! Fucking loser!"

Hearing Dmitri talk to me like I was nothing pissed me off and kinda hit me in the damn heart. My grandfather made plenty of money back in the day when we came to the states, he taught me everything he knew and I had plenty of success when I got older and started doing my own thing. I don't know what Dmitri was talking about calling me a nickel and dime hustler. I was the king before I got locked up and Tamar took all that away from me.

"Sy, just get out of my office. We have nothing more to talk about," Dmitri waved his hand dismissively like I was his maid or something. Fuckin' Italians didn't have respect for anyone and thought that blacks were worse than a piece of gum stuck to their shoe.

POW! POW!

Dmitri's eyes bucked open as he grabbed at the two holes that penetrated his chest and leaked dark red blood. He gasped for air, looked at me with apologetic eyes, then slumped over his desk.

I put my gun away, grabbed the set of keys that sat on his desk, and made my way over to his safe.

"Mr.---oh my God!" the assistant screamed.

I quickly pulled my hammer back out and fired at her but she ran away. I ran out of the office and into the hallway, looked both ways but didn't see her.

"Fuck!" I yelled.

I ran over to the banister, looked over the stair case, and spotted her running towards the front door.

POW! POW! POW! POW!

"Shit!" I yelled out.

One of the bullets penetrated her back causing her to hit the floor right in the entrance of the door. I shrugged my shoulders and went back into Dmitri's office to hit his safe.

"Muthafucka wanna talk to me like I'm some damn mutt!" I hissed as I unlocked the safe. My eyes lit up seeing the piles of money that lay in neat stacks. I grabbed every bit of it, stuffing as much as possible in my pockets, and the rest I carried away in my hands.

For good measure, I fired another shot into Dmitri, and made my way out of the office. If these muthafuckas wouldn't allow me to work for it then I would just take it. It made no difference to me.

****

I sat outside the hospital, with my guard on high alert. I knew that it would eventually get back to Dmitri's father that I killed him which meant I was working on borrowed time. It wouldn't be long before I would have an army of crazy ass Italians after me. Shit was not going the way I expected it to. My plan was beginning to unravel right in front of my face and there was nothing I could do to stop it. Tamar was still sitting on top, the only connection I had to getting where I wanted to be was lying dead in his upscale office. I'd unintentionally begun a war that I wasn't prepared to fight.

"Over here!" I yelled out of the crack in my window.

I unlocked my doors, looked around, and waited for him to get in. Soon as he shut the door, I cranked the car up and drove a few blocks down the road.

"Why haven't I heard from you? You took my money and just disappeared on me," I said parking behind a van.

"I did what you asked me to do. Apparently it worked cause they called me up here to give some damn blood for the lil' nigga."

"Give blood for what?" I asked wondering about the kids. When I cut Tamar's brake line, the last thing I wanted was for his shorties to get hurt. Hurting them meant hurting Rozalyn and that's not what I wanted at all. I hoped by some small lick of luck that I was able to repair things with her and we can move on with our lives. I really cared about shorty and wanted to see where things could go with her baby daddy out of the picture.

"One of the twins was hurt in an accident and apparently he lost a lot of blood. They having trouble finding a match and begged me to come up here."

"Damn, shorty was hurt?" I sighed. "Did you give blood?"

"Hell nah, this may be some kind of set up. You see all them niggas walking around outside. Those are his men and I ain't trying to walk into no ambush."

"I don't even know why you showed up in the first place. What's gonna happen if you try and give blood and they find out you not a match B? You're just gonna fuck up everything," I said shaking my head.

"There is still the possibility that the twins may be mine and I at least need to try. I can't have that on my shoulders."

I sighed, "I don't wanna take that chance. How about I give you another five racks to just go home and let them find another match."

I met Brandon back when he first got locked up for murdering his girlfriend. He was my cell mate for two months before he was transferred to a mental institution after being declared as being temporarily insane. Those two months that he was down, I learned everything I needed to know about Tamar and Rozalyn through him. The fact that they were no longer together, him having sex with Rozalyn right before she got pregnant with her twins, and the small possibility of them being his.

He displayed so much anger for Tamar that I knew he would be beneficial to me on the outside. As soon as he left the mental asylum, I paid him five grand, and then gave him another five grand to pay a tech at the lab to say that Tamar wasn't the father of the twins. It was possible that we didn't even have to go to the extreme of paying for a false test but I wanted to be certain that the results came back the way that I wanted them to.

The fact still remained that Brandon could be the father but then it was possible that he wasn't. I didn't want him going up in the hospital and giving blood and it came back that it wasn't a match. The goal was to put a dent in their relationship and ensure that they would never get back together. I wasn't so sure it had worked since Rozalyn never brought it up but I had a feeling it was why she had been so down lately.

"Look, now I'm thinking maybe it might be a good idea for you to try and give blood. If it comes back that you're not a match, then Tamar might start to believe that there was another man," I said now thinking that it might not be such a bad idea.

"Wasn't another fuckin' man!" Brandon yelled becoming visibly upset. He grasped the handle of the door and pushed the door open.

I laughed, "Yea okay. Just give blood and hit me up later. I got something else I need for you to do."

"Yea a'ight," Brandon got out of the car, looked around, and then made his way back to the hospital.

I would hate to have friends like him. I thought as I drove away.

18: Brandon

Honestly, I felt bad as fuck doing this shit but I had no other choice. I no longer wanted to hurt Tamar and definitely wasn't interested in seeing Rozalyn hurting. She'd been through enough with or without me being in the mix and didn't deserve to suffer anymore.

As much as I wanted to quit while I was ahead. I had to keep going because I needed the damn money. I'd lost everything when I got locked up and could barely afford to put a roof over my damn head. With the five grand that Sy paid me I was able to get a raggedy ass apartment, a bum ass sofa, and a few groceries. I hate the day I ever betrayed Tamar and wish I could take it all back. Sleeping with Rozalyn, killing Keylan, shit even killing Brittany. She was someone that truly loved me and I wish I would've recognized that instead of going after something that wasn't mine.

I know Tamar's heart wasn't forgiving of those that crossed him but I wished somehow I could mend things. I needed work bad and without Tamar approving me to do so I would never find it unless I worked for the opposing side. He had shit on lock in the South and everyone knew me and what I'd done so they wouldn't dare cross him. Sy had been my only option to get some type of money in my pocket. He'd told me to look him up when I touched down if I wanted to make some money and that's exactly what I did. I never expected him to use all the information I had stupidly given him to go after Tamar and Rozalyn. I just knew that he was going to use me to help him push some weight around but the fool was on that dumb shit just like I had been before being locked up.

"That sucka ass nigga is here."

I looked to my left and spotted a big bulky looking dude speak through an ear piece. He shot me a mug as I walked through the entrance of the hospital. I didn't know if coming here was a good idea or not. This all could've been a set up and I was just walking into a trap. The DNA test was supposed to read that Tamar wasn't the father of the twins but every time I called Rozalyn and asked about seeing the boys she told me that they were at Tamar's. I knew Tamar and knew that he wouldn't continue to take care of kids that weren't his. The fact that he has yet to come after me had me baffled.

If I wasn't the father and Tamar was, why the hell did Taron call me and ask if I could give blood? The shit wasn't making any sense to me but I guess I would soon find out what was what.

"This way," Taron said. He held a bag of ice to his lip, and ushered me through a set of double doors. I walked side by side with Taron until we made it to a room that had two hospital beds. I looked around and spotted Rozalyn in one corner and Tamar and a chick with freckles in another. I shook my head not knowing what the hell was going on. Rozalyn had a huge ass bandage on her forehead, Tamar had all kinds of gauzes wrapped around his left arm, and a big bandage across his exposed chest.

I attempted not to make eye contact with anyone but couldn't help but stare into the eyes of the woman that I loved more than anything in this world. Her beauty was beyond any woman that I'd ever seen. Even with the puffy, swollen eyes, she bore a look that just couldn't be touched.

"Nah nigga, keep your ass right there. Muthafuckin' nurse will be down in just a minute," Tamar said as he stood up from the chair he was sitting in.

I noticed one of the twins looking at me and wanted to go over and talk to him. He had an IV coming from his arm and a couple of other tubes coming from his mouth and nose. Looking at him, I honestly didn't see any resemblance to myself. He looked just like Rozalyn's older brother Zavier, damn near a splitting image of him. I didn't see me, Tamar, nor Rozalyn in his features.

"I---I just wanted to talk to him. He mine right?" I asked nervously.

"He might share your blood but he will never be yours! All I need is for you to let these folks take your blood and move the fuck around!"

"So, you just gonna use me to save the lil' nigga but I can't see them and get to know them. Man fuck that!" I protested.

"Brandon please--"Rozalyn stepped in but Tamar jumped in front of her and faced me.

"Nah Rozalyn, you not about to beg this coward to do a muthafuckin thing! He gonna do this shit or else they gonna carry his ass down to that muthafuckin' morgue. His choice!"

I looked at Tamar trying not flinch at his words. I knew that he meant every word and could make it happen. His goons were posted all around the hospital and I'm sure all of them were heavily armed. I was going to give blood anyway but I at least wanted to barter my way into the twins' lives if they were indeed mine.

"We're ready."

I looked over my shoulder and spotted a heavy set nurse dressed in blue scrubs with a huge smile on her face. I backed away from Tamar before following behind the nurse.   "Go with him and make sure he do this shit," I heard Tamar say before I exited the room.

Taron went with us as the nurse took me to the lab they had within the hospital. My legs felt like spaghetti as I made my way over to a chair and was instructed to hold my hand out. I didn't know what would happen if I wasn't a match. Tamar would no longer need me and could easily order his goons to take me out the moment I stepped foot out of this hospital. I thought about unmasking Sy and letting Tamar know what was up but then that could go either way.

"Do you know your blood type?" The nurse asked as she grabbed my index finger.

"Think I'm AB negative," I replied.

"Are you sure?" she asked with a raise of her eyebrow.

"Yea, I'm sure."

She looked at me, shrugged, and then poked my finger with a small needle. She pushed down on the finger until there was a good amount of blood and scooped it up into a tiny tube.

"Give me just a minute and let me double check it."

I nodded my head and looked down at the floor. Taron stood over me like a watch dog waiting for me to make one wrong move.

"How is lil' dude doing?" I asked trying to make conversation.

"Fuck happened to you?" Taron asked ignoring my question.

"You see them people said I was crazy," I said with a smirk.

"You ain't fuckin' crazy! You knew exactly what you was doing!"

"Excuse me, but he's not a match either. I will get with the blood bank to see where we are on getting the blood for Zavier," the nurse said as she sadly looked at Taron.

"What the fuck is going on?" Taron wondered aloud. "Ma'am you sure that his mother can't donate blood? And if not then this is supposed to be the father, why wouldn't he be a match. Is he not the father?"

I chocked back a glob of spit and silently awaited her answer hoping that she wouldn't say anything that would get me killed.

"Paternity cannot be established through blood type but AB type can only give blood to someone that is AB as well. The mother definitely cannot since she is RH positive and Zavier is A positive. One of his parents should be a match."

"Okay but they're not, so what are you saying?" Taron asked.

"I'm not saying anything. Paternity cannot be established through just blood type. All I know is that at least one of Zavier's parents should have a matching factor. Let's go speak with the doctor and see what he wants to do next."

Taron was so busy talking with the nurse that he was no longer paying me any mind. I used that as an opportunity to slip out unnoticed. I rushed out of the lab, raced down the hall, and out of the hospital. Once I was outside, I pulled my hoodie over my head, and moved sleekly through the night. After tonight, I'm letting Sy know that I'm not helping him do shit else. If he wanted to take Tamar down, he would have to do it on his own.

"Aye, B!"

I looked up and noticed a familiar face standing a few feet in front of me. He was dressed in all black with a hoodie very similar to mine. A cigarette hung from his lip, and a pistol idled by his side.

"Black?" I questioned now recognizing him from a slight glare that shined onto his face from the street light.

"Yep, what's good fammo? I've been dying for this moment youngin'," Black said blowing out a cloud of smoke.

Black is a known killer from out of Dallas, who has knocked off more people than the war in Iraq. He has done plenty of work in Atlanta and was well respected all over the damn globe for jobs he has done. It didn't surprise me that he was here; now that Keylan was gone Tamar needed more cut-throat goons on his team, and who better than Black.

"Let Tae know I got some info for him that I know he'll benefit from," I stated nervously. My eyes darted around as I plotted my escape route in my head. I wouldn't have much room to get away but I would try. Black's aim is superior and I knew he wouldn't miss me but there was no way I would just lay down like some coward.

"Boss man ain't trying to hear shit and neither am I. You took away something very precious to a lot of people youngin'. I've been itching to get at you for real. Boss man called me and told me he needed me to handle this because he didn't have the heart to do it, so I came running," Black explained.

I nodded my head, backed away a couple of feet, and then turned around and took off running as fast as possible.

POW! POW! POW!

I felt each bullet as they entered my back and sent me stumbling over to the ground. I got up on my knees, tried to crawl away, but was kicked in my stomach and tossed onto my back. I looked up at Black and didn't see an inch of innocence in his eyes. I'd known this dude for many years and knew he wouldn't have any mercy on me. Black was rotted to the core; his heart was black, and made of steel. I contemplated pleading with him to allow me to make it another day but knew that was exactly what he wanted. Blood seeped through my mouth and nose and I began to gasp for air.

"Go to sleep nigga!" Black yelled before he emptied the remainder of the clip into me.

POW! POW! POW! POW!

19: Rozalyn

Things were not looking good for Zavier and I wasn't quite sure how I should feel right now. I had a rare blood type and couldn't even do what was needed to save my own damn son's life. No one was looking to be a match for him and waiting on the blood bank made me feel like a kid waiting for Christmas. Taron had Tamar believing that there was another man involved that could possibly be the father of Zyir and Zavier but that was the least bit true. All the kind words, all the begging that Tamar did the other night had completely gone out the window. He'd called me so many bitches, sluts, and whores in the last twenty four hours that I started to believe the shit was true. If Brandon wasn't the father and Tamar wasn't either then who the hell was? I know for a fact that I didn't sleep with anyone else around the time I got pregnant.

"Hey baby. How are they?" Cheryl asked as she met me half way down her drive way.

"Umm, Tamarion and Zyir are doing okay. They ran all kinds of test on them and determined they were well enough to come home," I said feeling all kinds of emotions rush through me.

"And Zavier?" Cheryl questioned with a sense of sadness in her voice.

"Not too good. He has lost a lot of blood, the blood bank is low on blood for him and we are just waiting to get some in."

"Oh God. Yea, Ron told me they were having a hard time finding blood. What's going on with---well I know it's not my business but Tamar isn't the father of the twins Rozalyn?"

I shook my head no and broke out into a horrendous cry. Just hearing another person speak my shame aloud hurt me to the core. I know everyone was looking at me with very unforgiving eyes especially at a time like this.

"Well what about Brandon, Rozalyn? Taron told me he was out. Did anyone try and get in contact with him about giving blood?" Cheryl asked sounding just as confused as the situation.

"He couldn't I don't know what's going on---Tamar is thinking I slept with someone else but I didn't Mrs. Cheryl---I didn't!" I cried.

She took me into her arms and we walked both boys into the house. Cheryl and I discussed everything that happened at the hospital last night over hot green tea that she'd made. She told me not to worry about anything and that God would make a way out of no way. I wanted to believe her but with my son on the verge of death; it was a hard thing to do.

I sat with Cheryl and listened to her preach to me about the many mistakes I've made in my life. She explained to me the beauty about being given a second chance and how a person should never take advantage of them. Hearing all this got me to thinking about the other night at the restaurant with Tamar. We'd been given so many chances to work on our relationship and be a family as we should but each time we both somehow ruined it. Tamar asked me to be with him again and I flat out told him no, walked away, and didn't even look back.

I honestly felt that all of our chances had run out. What more could I offer to Tamar besides more heartache and pain and him doing the same to me. My main goal was to start focusing more on my children and my relationship with Messiah. I know that I could be a good woman and love someone the way that I want to be loved but I just had to give it a shot. Men like Messiah don't come around often and I needed to see to it that he didn't get away from me.

***

"Thank you for letting me use your truck," I said to Tamar as I handed him his keys.

He and Kari sat bundled up in the corner of Zavier's room, looking like the world's greatest couple. That bitch hasn't left his side since she found out he and I were in the same hospital and I needed him. He believed there was another party involved that could have fathered my twins and I had to let him know that wasn't so.

"Can I talk to you for a moment?"

Tamar looked at me like I was bugging him and the bitch Kari had the nerve to suck her teeth at me. I crossed my arms over my chest and patiently waited for Tamar to make a move. I know he did not expect for me to talk in front of this evil, conniving ass bitch.

"In private please," I said becoming frustrated.

Tamar got up from his chair and exited the room. I followed behind him and frowned once I noticed him going to the elevators.

"Tae, I only need a couple of minutes. Right here is fine," I sighed placing my hands on my hips.

"Well I'm about to go outside and fire up this blunt. You wanna talk, you can talk then."

I rolled my eyes and couldn't help but shoot Tamar a friendly smirk as I followed him onto the small, convoluted elevator. He leaned against the back doors and I pressed the button to take us to the first floor. Once we were off the elevator and outside, Tamar reached behind his ear and pulled out a blunt. He lit it up, took a couple of tokes, and offered it in my direction.

I took the blunt from his hand and took two light puffs from it before handing it back. I found a relaxing place against a pole, crossed my arms over my chest, and looked in Tamar's direction. He looked so relaxed, so calm, and so--so much like the family man that I've always wanted. I normally saw him so serious and always in game mode that I didn't even know this mellow side even existed.

"Look, I just wanted to say regardless of what happened with this blood situation. You and Brandon were the only ones that I was with. I know for a fact that there is no other possibility---"

I stopped mid-sentence when I saw a handful of doctors and nurses rushing towards the emergency room doors, pushing a man on a gurney. The individual only caught my attention because he was wearing clothes similar to what Brandon had on last night. As they came closer, I realized that my eyes hadn't been playing tricks on me. My hand went over my mouth seeing the bloody bullet holes that covered his clothing and flesh. Tamar caught the look of horror on my face so he turned to look as well. His reaction wasn't as shocking as mine; he more angered and flat out baffled. He flicked the blunt across the concrete, grabbed his cell phone from his pocket, and stormed off into the night.

Instinctively I chased behind the doctors and nurses that were pushing Brandon into the hospital. I wanted to know what happened to him, was he going to be okay, and if there was anything I could do to help. I mean he was my kid's father, right? I had a right to feel sympathetic and scared for him. Right? Confused tears ran down my face as I followed behind the army of staff, trying to unravel the codes that they spoke amongst each other.

"Excuse me!" I called out but they were all too busy to even hear me.

After watching them disappear through the busy double doors of the hospital, I made my way to the nurse's desk ready to see what information I could get on Brandon. There was only one nurse working behind the desk at the moment, a black chick with long fake nails, and a super long, thick weave. She was a very attractive female and seemed like she had a lot of sense.

"Can I help you?" she asked as she rolled her chair closer to me.

"No, she's good."

I looked over my shoulder to see Tamar standing over me. His nostrils flared repeatedly as he gently pulled me away from the nurse's desk.

"Your child is upstairs fighting for his life and you down here worrying about this muthafucka!" Tamar said through somewhat gritted teeth.

I could only stare at Tamar knowing that this was no coincidence. Brandon had showed his face last night and after finding out he wasn't able to donate blood; he was shot down. This had only one person's name on it and I knew for sure I was looking at him.

20: Tamar

I sat back fiddling with my thumbs as all kinds of thoughts rushed through my head. Black was supposed to have handled Brandon, murked him, snatched his lights out, and the muthafucka was still breathing a whole fuckin' day later. I'd called Black's cell phone thirty times in the past hour and have yet to receive an answer from him. I was very tempted to make my way over to the trauma unit and finish Brandon off my damn self. When I found out that he wasn't able to donate blood to his shorty — my shorty, I put the order in to have him killed the moment he walked out of this hospital since the nigga was no longer needed. I hope he didn't think because he was possibly the father of the twins that I was gonna let him slide for all the bullshit he's done. Although I couldn't pull the trigger myself, it was a must that he went down. There was no way possible I could have his conniving ass roaming the same streets as me again. Just seeing him yesterday for the brief moment that we were in each other's presence, I knew for a fact that he was up to something. I had no idea what but I knew that I couldn't let him make it away from this hospital.

Sadly, the fool was fighting for his pitiful life as doctors did everything in their power to save him. I know for a fact I saw at least four to five bullet holes in this nigga so he had to have bled out profusely and on top of that the shit happened on yesterday evening, but yet he was still breathing.

Just how many lives does this green-eyed bastard have? I wondered to myself.

I sat here and thought about all the times this fool had escaped death since he'd been a child and really wondered if he had some type of angel watching over him. I know that I've been shot, shot at, stabbed, and everything else but Brandon has been through the trenches and back and still seems to come out just fine. But I will worry about that later.

I sat a few feet away from Zavier's bed half-way listening to Chalo, one of Dmitri's workers explain to me how he found Dmitri and his assistant rotting away in Dmitri's mansion and how he felt that I was responsible. Dmitri's safe had been ripped off, his surveillance videos were missing, and whoever was accountable for his death pretty much knew the ins and outs of Dmitri's home. I vaguely watched Chalo's lips move as he spit threat after threat to me, never showing him any emotion, any weakness, or even a sign that I cared about what he was telling me. Showing emotion would somehow signify guilt and that I didn't have. Dmitri was like a father to me and to hear that he was dead was devastating but I wasn't the one responsible. I didn't have anything to gain from Dmitri dying nor did I have anything to lose. He is or never was a threat to me so why on earth would I kill him? He called me a thief and cut me off but in the end it turned out to be the most beneficial thing that he'd ever done for me.

Chalo and I have never had problems; his presence here was like a present to me. He was here to give fair warning that soon someone would be coming for me and if they had to hurt my family to get to me; they would.

"Chalo, you know I didn't do this right?" I asked finally breaking my silence after an hour long.

"I don't know what to believe anymore Tamar. There was the accusation of you stealing and then this--I don't know. All I know is that Donald is very upset and he wants someone to pay. He doesn't care who," Chalo further explained. "He says that he wants you to come and see him and if you don't he will send the army after you. You know that he is not a violent person and that is why he is giving you until after the service to come and talk to him like a man."

I chuckled, "This shit is crazy as fuck."

I shook my head in disbelief and instantly began thinking where I could take my family to get them out of harms way. This shit seemed as if it would never stop and honestly I was getting tired of it all, constantly looking over my shoulder, sleeping with a gun under my pillow, and always looking at every muthafucka as a threat. I think I've finally reached the point where the bad outweighed the good. The only good thing about this game is the money, power, and respect I got but when shit kept falling into my lap and spilling over into my family's lap all the money, power, and respect didn't matter.

"Look, preciate you coming by Chalo but I have nothing to say to Donald except for that I am sorry for his loss. I had nothing to do with Dmitri's death but if he insists that I did and he comes after me then I guess we have a problem."

"Then you should come--"

"I'm not coming to do a muthafucking thing!" I bellowed. The sound of my voice echoing off the walls caused Zavier to stir a little in his sleep. I moved closer to his side, grabbed his hand, and stared intently in Chalo's direction. "Like I said, let Donald know that I am sorry for his loss."

Chalo stood up from his chair, reached out to shake my hand but I only stared at it like he'd been infected with the plague. Nigga would be gunning for me later so there was no need to exchange pleasantries like everything was cool when it wasn't. I watched as Chalo exited the hospital room, then immediately picked up my cell phone to dial Black's number again; this time he answered on the first ring.

"Aye, I need to see you at the hospital—now."

                                    ***

"Oh my God, you scared the fuck outta of me!" Kari yelled as she placed her hand over her rapidly rising chest.

"Didn't mean to, what are you doing?" I asked getting a glimpse of the magazine that Kari tried to slide between the couch cushion.

"Nothing, just reading and catching up on a few movies."

I moved over to the couch and took a seat next to Kari, pulling the magazine from between the cushion, "Brides?" I questioned noticing that she was reading a magazine dealing with weddings.

"Yea, Donica left it in my car so I just started reading it. It's nothing," Kari laughed nervously.

"It's addressed to you. I thought that I told you to chill on that marriage shit," I said with a frown.

"Well that was a couple of months ago. I figured since we've been spending so much time together that you may have changed your mind."

"Nah, why would I have changed my mind? You left the hospital the moment you got a chance, like it was killing you to be there and you haven't even called one time since you left to see how my shorty was doing!"

"I stayed by your side the whole time and only left after I saw you let Rozalyn use your fucking car and besides he's not even your damn kid! Why should you care?"

It took everything in me not to slap the shit out of Kari and spit in her damn face! The bitch must've lost her damn mind to say some foul ass shit like that to me, either that or she just didn't know what kinda man I was. I've taken care of the twins since they were fuckin' born so as long as I was alive I wasn't about to allow another man to care for them.

"Look, I need you to pack your things and leave my house. It's over Kari," I said, my tone stiff and serious.

"What? Wait a minute, what do you mean it's over?" Kari slid to the end of the couch and stared at the side of my face.

"It's over. I need my wife back and I can't get her if I'm laid up with you every day," I sighed.

"You say that like it's nothing! What do you mean you need your wife back? What the fuck Tamar? Don't do this to me! No, you cannot do this to me! I left my husband to be with you!"

"Didn't nobody tell you to leave that nigga man! Look, I got some shit I gotta handle and then I'm going back to the hospital to be with my son. I need you to be out of here by six pm tonight. I'll send Black through here to make sure of it," I stood up from the couch and proceeded to leave the room.

Kari jumped up and grabbed my arm, pulled me around to face her, and dropped down to her knees. I looked down at her shaking my head, hoping that she was not about to start begging me. My mind had been made up for weeks now and nothing was going to be able to change that. I tried to go the gentlemen route and get Rozalyn to come home, be romantic, take her out to dinner, eat her out, and then practically beg her to come home but she wanted to continue to play crazy. Now it was time that I brought her home by force. Being that I got the Italian mob coming after me, I knew that I could force her on a vacation where we could spend a few days alone. A few days was all I needed to convince her that I'd changed, and changed for the better.

"Kari, shit--" I groaned. I titled my head back in pure pleasure when Kari swallowed every inch of me into her mouth. I wanted to push her away and let her know that this shit wasn't going to work but the feeling was just too good. Kari's head game was spectacular and one that just couldn't be passed up. I gripped the back of her head, pounding my dick into her throat, making her gag a little before she pushed me away.

"I hate when you do that!" she yelled crawling over to me.

"I hate when you run, turn around," I ordered.

Kari happily pulled her shorts and panties off and eagerly obeyed my command. She turned around while on all fours, tooted her ass up in the air, and patiently waited for me to enter her. I got down on my knees and slid deep inside of her, spreading her butt cheeks apart as I slowly stroked her pussy. Her muscles tightened, pulling me in with each stroke I made and getting wetter with each dive.

"Yes daddy! Yes! Give me that dick baby! Give it to me!" Kari yelled as she threw her ass back at me.

"Shit, tighten that pussy up!" I said slapping her on the ass.

"This is your pussy baby! It's yours! It's not going anywhere!"

Hearing Kari yell that shit out made me want to hurry up and get my nut. I knew if we went this route that she would began to think everything was okay and would go back to normal but this was it. This was the last time I was going inside of her pussy and I meant that shit to the fullest. Kari hasn't done anything for me all of this time that we've been together besides please me sexually; but the sex was just okay. It wasn't like she blew my mind every time we were together that I was afraid to let her go.

"Aaghh shit," I said pulling my dick out and blowing all over Kari's back. "Six o'clock."

I slapped Kari on the ass once more before standing up and putting my dick back up. I went to reach for my keys, my hat, and was about to head out of the door when I was knocked in the back of my head with something hard. The blow caused me to hit the floor hard, I was then kicked in my side, followed by a kick to my face.

"Nigga, you think you just gonna leave me like this with no consequences! I held your ass down when that bitch broke your damn heart!" Kari yelled.

"Crazy ass bitch," I spit. Blood leaked from my busted lip as I went to get up from the floor. Kari came at me again but this time I grabbed her with one arm and flung her across the room where she slid across the floor and hit the couch. I looked down on the floor and noticed that Kari had took a lamp from the end table and hit me with it, there were pieces of it were scattered across the floor with remnants of blood on it. "Bitch, put your hands on me again and I promise you'll regret it!"

"Tae, you cannot do this to me! What do I have to do? Please don't do this to me. I love you!" Kari cried as she crawled in my direction again.

"Keep your crazy ass away from me man! Hurry up and get your shit and get the fuck out!"

"Where am I supposed to go? You can't just put me--"

I walked out of the family room and headed towards the door to leave. Soon as I got in the car, I would let Black know to come through here and make sure that bitch left with no problems. She better be lucky I allowed her ass to live after she knocked me over the head with that damn lamp.

I reached for the door knob when Kari slapped my hand away and grabbed me by my arm. Had I known she was gonna go this crazy I would've told her ass to get out over the phone. I jerked my arm away from Kari and tried to pull the door open again, when a sharp stinging pain hit my wrist. Blood shot from my wrist like a water faucet, down my arm, and onto the floor. It took me a moment to notice that Kari had slit me open with a knife that she'd grabbed in her fight to try and stop me from leaving. I walked into her direction, with each step seeming harder and harder to make. Kari wore a sleek grin on her face that seemed to get blurrier by the second. I reached out to grab her but everything went black once I fell to the floor face first.

21: Latoya

I made my way into Applebee's and looked around for my party before pointing them out to the hostess, letting her know that I didn't need to be seated. I was slightly disappointed in seeing that there were two people here instead of one and almost turned around and walked out of the restaurant. Once I made it to the table, I gave a fake ass smile and took a seat across from them, folding my arms across my chest, and showing that I didn't appreciate this shit at all.

"Toya, what's up? This my fiancé Journey, Journey this is Toya," Taron said as he introduced the two of us.

"Look, when I said that I would meet you, I don't remember saying for you to bring anybody else with you," I blatantly said as I eyed Journey.

"This is my fiancé Toya, she wants to get to know Keymani just as much as I want to."

"First Keymani needs to get to know you before she can get to know anyone else," I stood up from the table now feeling as if I had been completely disrespected. Taron had no right to bring this bitch up in here, the fact that she was here made me aware that the only reason he finally agreed to be in his daughter's life is because of her.

Taron being the father of Keymani was never supposed to happen. The unfortunate event took place on a very vulnerable night when I'd gone down to the club looking for Keylan. I was sick and tired of not being able to spend time with Keylan, him always putting his work before me, and the fact that he was still not ready to have a family. Taron ended up being the person I leaned on, after smoking a couple of blunts and having too many cups of brown liquor things went way further than they should have. I never once thought that he could be the father of my child and even when I found out that Keylan nor Kevin was the father; I didn't even think twice about Taron until months later. Even then it took me a while to contact him because I was too ashamed of what everyone would think of me. I'd already slept with Kevin behind Keylan's back and now I had also slept with practically his damn brother. I had to get out of my selfishness and do what was right for Keymani, she needed her father in her life no matter what anyone thought about me and what I did. I didn't want to deprive her of that opportunity just because I didn't want to be embarrassed.

"Toya, the reason why I am here is because Taron and I are getting married soon and I want to be a part of Keymari's life. We actually are wondering if you would allow her to come and stay with us," Journey said.

I looked at Journey, held my breath, and tried to calm myself down. She is a real pretty girl, brown skinned, nice weave, pretty straight teeth and from what I can tell she has an okay shape. I looked from Taron to Journey waiting to see if one of them were gonna speak up and redeem themselves from what this bitch just said.

"First of all Mrs. Journey, my daughter's name is Keymani, not fuckin Keymari!" I yelled. "And second of all, why the fuck would I let my child come and stay with two damn strangers?"

I stood up from my chair and gave Taron one last look, not able to believe that this big sexy nigga couldn't do, think, or speak for himself. I looked into his brown eyes, studied his full succulent lips, and smiled at him weakly, "When you're really ready to see Keymani, give me a call!"

"Ghetto bitch," Journey muttered as I walked away.

I stopped mid stride, turned around to look at her, and then sashayed back in her direction. Taron hurriedly jumped from his seat and came to stand in between the two of us. He towered over me standing at more than six feet tall with a muscular build.

"Maybe I can get your damn brother to talk some sense into you, because you obviously don't have any. You better get that bitch before my ghetto ass fucks her up," I shoved Taron slightly in the chest and this time walked off for good.

Once I got outside and unarmed the alarm on my Jag, I noticed Taron coming towards me with pure speed in his steps. I hurriedly jumped in my car and cranked it before he could make it over to me. Just as I put the car in gear, Taron knocked on my window, and began to pull on the handle.

"Move nigga before I run your big ass over!" I yelled through the closed window.

"Open the door! Don't you drive off!" he yelled hitting on the window.

I placed the car in park, rolled my window down, and crossed my arms over my chest pouting as Taron leaned inside the window. The Sean John cologne he was wearing had me drooling at the mouth and my pussy sensationally wet. It had been a very long time since I've had sex since I only got it from Kevin when he and his fiancé Kyla were into it. Now that he knows that Taron is the father of my daughter he's already called and said that he doesn't ever wanna see or talk to me again. Since I inherited all of Keylan's property and his money it's hard for me to find a suitable guy that wants to be with me for me and not for what I have. I also had to be careful about who I allowed around my child being that Kevin is the only man she knows.

"Look, I only brought her to prove that you and I were not messing around. She thinks that I cheated and still is cheating but I've been telling her that's not true. All that shit about having Keymani coming to live with me was not my idea," Taron said.

"Well next time leave her at home. I don't have time for your insecure women," I huffed.

"Women?" he chuckled. "Nah, it's not like that. I really wanna see my daughter and get to know her. So if it's cool with you I would like to come through there tomorrow and spend the day with her."

"As long as your bitch stays at home, that's fine with me."

"Be nice, but okay she will stay at home," Taron leaned in and pressed his soft lips against my cheek; a feeling that caused me to damn near melt into my leather seats. I didn't give a damn that he was about to get married, I was horny as hell and was not allowing Taron to leave until I got another taste of that. I needed some regular dick in my life and what better choice than the father of my child.

22: Rozalyn

I lie in bed with Messiah's arms roaming all over my body. Being able to have him hold me after sex and not rush off into the streets is a wonderful thing. I wasn't used to this kind of love but I could damn sure get used to it. I rolled over onto my side and faced Messiah, sucked his bottom lip into my mouth, and then gave him a sensual smile.

"I think I'm really starting to fall for you," I said kissing him once more.

"Well you know that I been fell for you. I'm just waiting for you," Messiah said as he rubbed his hand up and down my leg.

"I'm getting there. A little more time together," I sat up I'm the bed and reached for the blunt that Messiah left sitting on the night stand. I took the lighter, fired it up, and took a deep puff from it.

"Does Tae give you money every month to pay your bills?" Messiah asked.

"No, I told you that already," I said and took another toke from the blunt.

"I'm just saying he gotta be helping you with your bills 'cause you don't ask me for shit."

"I pay my own bills. I manage my money well so there is no need for me to ask anyone for anything. If I learned anything from Tamar, it was to manage my funds appropriately."

"Oh yea, stacking up all the cash and stashing it under the floorboards and inside the mattress huh?" Messiah chuckled "I know all that money Tamar gots he probably runs out of hiding spots huh?"

I passed the blunt over to Messiah and got up from the bed. His line of questioning was starting to make me feel uncomfortable just like it did the day he brought me home from the hospital.

"Where you going?"

"It's time for me to get back." I quipped while grabbing my clothing from the floor.

"Wait, come here!" Messiah reached me but I pulled away.

"I gotta go!" I fussed. I pulled my panties on and then pulled on my jeans buttoning them up as Messiah continued to kiss all over my back.

"Just five more minutes, just five more," Messiah said trying to pull my jeans back down.

"No, I gotta get back to the hospital with my baby," I turned around and kissed Messiah, pulled his bottom lip into my mouth again, and then backed away from him.

"How is the little man doing?" Messiah asked finally giving in and pulling up his pants.

"He's doing better. He finally got the blood from the bank and slowly progressing. Hopefully he will be good enough to go home soon," I said pulling my shirt over my head and grabbing my purse.

Messiah and I decided to meet up at a motel a couple of hours ago being I haven't seen him since the day he brought me home from the hospital after I'd bumped my head. I missed him and really needed to get a little breath of fresh air after being in that damn hospital hour after hour with Tamar. I couldn't stand the way he constantly stared at me for hours without saying a word or even blinking his damn eye. With him you never knew what was on his mind but somehow I knew he was silently plotting my death. He was pissed that I was so determined to find out what happened to Brandon but didn't give a damn about him when he was facing death.

Unfortunately, Brandon didn't make it and that was another reason I needed out of that place. I'd never wanted to see Brandon dead no matter what he had done. I just wished that he'd spent more time in jail, enough time that would allow everyone to heal over the two deaths he caused. I struggled with my emotions after finding out about Brandon's death and as soon as Tamar turned his back, I rushed out of the room, and got out of the hospital as quickly as possible. I planned to spend some alone time but figured getting some dick would definitely put my mind to ease.

"So, when am I going to see you again?" Messiah asked while walking over to me.

"I don't know, with Zavier being in the hospital and then Zyir and Marion being at their grandmother's; I really don't have a lot of time to do anything."

"Damn, it's like that?" Messiah gripped my face into both of his hands and kissed me. He then released his hands from my cheeks, and roamed his hands over my body, finally resting them on my butt. We tongued each other for minutes before I finally pushed him away and attempted to leave the room. Messiah grabbed me by my wrist and pulled me into his arms once more. "Why haven't you worn the bracelet that I brought you?"

I looked down at my wrist remembering that Tamar had snatched it off a few days ago. I tried to think of a legitimate excuse as to why I wasn't wearing it before answering.

"Oh, umm, it kept getting caught in Zavier's hair so I took it off. I'll be sure to put it back on today," I said with a faint smile.

"Yea, I wanna see how good my money looks on you," Messiah kissed me once more and finally let me go. I blew him a kiss, left him with a warm smile, and headed out of the motel room.

****

Once I made it to the hospital, I saw the new guy Black seated in a chair outside of Zavier's room along with a thick dark-skinned chick. They were so deep into conversation that neither of them noticed me walk up.

"Hey," I said to the both of them.

"What's up Rozalyn? This is my girl Xenya, Xenya this my boss man's----umm his baby moms," Black said.

I gave each of them a smile and proceeded to walk into Zavier's room when Black stopped me.

"Have you talked to Tamar? I've been calling him but no answer," Black asked with a look of concern.

"Nah, I haven't talked to him since I left here a couple of hours ago. Let me try and call him," I said pulling out my cell phone.

The line trilled in my ear until the voice mail picked up. I hit the end button and did the same routine over and over again, finally hanging up calling the house phone.

"Hello," Kari asked.

"Hey Kari, I was trying to get in contact with Tamar. Is he there or have you seem him?" I asked in a slow, subtle tone.

"That's your fuckin' husband! You tell me if you've seen him! He isn't married to me, he's married to you!" Kari screamed through the phone causing me to frown in disgust.

"Kari, can you just let him know---"

"I'm not letting him know shit! Bastard wants to leave me for you! Like your young ass-"

I heard the phone being slammed down onto the receiver but could still hear Kari in the background. She was rambling on and on about her and Tamar and continuously let out a psycho sounding scream after every few words she spat.

"What's going on?" Black asked.

"You might need to get over to Tae's house. Listen at this crazy bitch," I said handing the phone to Black who'd already stood attentively and on guard.

Black placed his ear to the phone and immediately his face scrunched up into a frown. His caramel skin turned practically a reddish purple, his hand was balled up onto a tight fist, and his jaws tightened in fury. I backed away not sure what to expect while his girlfriend Xenya, consoled him by rubbing his back. I took in Xenya's exotic features, noticing how beautiful she was. Her dark skin glimmered; looking as if someone sprinkled glitter all over her. Her eyes were sorta like mine but she wasn't mixed with anything. She wore a lace front wig that was professionally done. Had I not been somewhat of a stylist I would've never known that it was wig being it had been done so perfectly. She had a full set of lips, the height of a model, but not the body type. She was very curvaceous but it looked great on her. Looking at her and looking at Black, I wondered what she saw in him. He was so homely and broke looking and everything about her exuded class.

Black handed me my cell phone and then pulled out his. He made a call and immediately started yelling the minute whoever he called answered. He kissed Xenya several times on the lips and rushed out of the hospital without so much as a word to either of us.

I left Xenya standing outside the room and went and sat next to Zavier's bed. He had his eyes open and stared at me for a few moments before looking at the cartoons on the t.v. Leaning towards him, I kissed him several times on his cheek and thank God that he was okay now. Things could have definitely been worse and I was more than happy to see that it wasn't.

Zavier was known to unbuckle his seat belt anytime he seen something in the car that he wanted but couldn't get to. Tamar fussed at him all the time about it and I'd even gotten on him as well. That particular morning of the accident, Zavier apparently pulled his seatbelt apart again and when they crashed he went flying out of his seat, into the front seat, where he hit the dashboard. The blow he took caused him to have a few broken bones and some internal bleeding. Each day doctors expected him to make a full recovery and soon he would be ready to go home.

I pulled his hand into mine and looked up and saw Xenya leaning against the door frame, "You can come in."

"I didn't want to scare him. He's so gorgeous," Xenya said as she took a seat nearby.

"Thank you." We sat in silence for a few moments before the silence began to kill me. I was beginning to worry about Tamar and Kari. I didn't miss the bitterness in Kari's voice and the psycho tone. I knew Tamar could hold his own but that bitch sounded real flipped like she suddenly lost all her marbles.

"So Xenya, what part of Atlanta do y'all live in?" I asked to take my mind off all the possible things that could be going wrong.

"Oh we don't live in Atlanta, we live in Dallas, Texas," she answered.

"Oh, I thought Tamar told me he met Black in Atlanta."

"I'm sure they did. He used to live there a few years back but he's originally from Dallas."

"Oh ok, I see," hearing somewhat of accent from her.

"Yea, he told me that he was only going to be out here a couple of weeks but now finding out that it might be a lot longer," Xenya sighed.

"You ready to go back home huh?"

"Something like that."

Since Xenya didn't seem to want to talk, I decided that I would   patiently   wait   to   hear   something   from   Black   or hopefully Tamar.

23: Messiah

I hid out in a wooded area about a half of mile away from Tamar's home. Using a set of binoculars, I looked on as paramedics and two police cars rushed through the secured gate and down the drive way to the mini mansion. I could only wonder what was going on and could only hope that it was Tamar they were coming to get. I'd been ducked off waiting to get in contact with Brandon so that I could set my plan into motion. He was the only close enough to Tamar that could get me what I needed in order to bring Tamar down.

I hadn't slept since Donald fired me and I killed Dmitri. Part of me didn't want to let Tamar out of my sight for one little minute but then half of me knew that eventually the Italians would come for me. It wouldn't be long before the back up on the surveillance was pulled and my ass was running for my life. I gave myself a week at the most to find out what I could about Tamar, take his paper, kill him, and get out of town. With the kind of money Tamar had, I could easily go to the Virgin Islands and live a damn good life with a few bad bitches if Rozalyn chose not to join me.

"Oh shit!" I eagerly stood up from my hiding spot, pulled the binoculars closer to my eyes and spotted Tamar being rushed onto the back of the ambulance. I was really getting sick of this nigga and starting to think he was a real live cat; twice I'd attempted to kill him and each time failed. The first time I put a homemade bomb under his truck while he was doing business at the courthouse, but unfortunately he had a remote starter and the bomb blew up prematurely on injuring him. The last time I cut his brake line only expecting for him to be in the car alone and not with his children. I was happy that the kids had not been hurt too bad but was truly upset that Tamar came through with just a few scratches.

"I gotta get in that house," I said to myself as I moved a couple of inches forward still keeping my eyes on the ambulance.

His whole team of security was so occupied in watching the ambulance pull off with their boss and the wild haired bitch the police pulled out shortly afterwards. I inched closer and closer to the home that was just down a bushy hill from where I was standing.

The closer and closer I got, the more confident I became that I was going to get inside. It seemed as if I had picked the perfect day to stand guard outside of Tamar's big ass home. I was about one hundred feet from the back door when my phone began to ring with Rozalyn's ring tone. I quickly took the cell phone out of my pocket and answered it, "Hello."

"Where are you? I need you!" Rozalyn frantically screamed.

"What's wrong with you? Where are you?" I asked and began to break into a sweat hearing the fear in her voice.

"They're making me--in---and the boys!" she said but the line was breaking up.

"Yo mama, I can't hear you! Repeat that!" I yelled.

"Dal--and--tonight! Hurry!"

Beep! Beep! Beep!

I pulled the phone away from my ear seeing that the call failed between Rozalyn and me. I couldn't hear shit she was saying but knew I needed to get to the hospital to see what was up or--did I? I'd never been so close to Tamar's home, so close that I could literally feel my pockets fattening.

I decided to wait until after I got into the house to find out what was wrong with Rozalyn. I mean she is at a hospital and if it was something serious; they could help her. I had to get this money from Tae, I just had to. This nigga was living good and it was all because of my hard work. I started this shit and if it wasn't for me he would still be living in the hood in Atlanta some damn where.

I made it to the gate, looked around trying to figure out just how I could jump over. The gate had to be over ten feet tall and was made of iron steel that I know would kill my ass if I landed on it the wrong way.

"Shit!" I wiped sweat from my forehead, and then leaned over with both hands on my knees. Tamar had definitely well thought this shit out when picking this house out. Anyone crazy enough to jump over would more than likely end up hurt or dead, but fuck it I was about to try.

I pulled my white Ralph Lauren shorts up and grab a hold of the gate ready to climb over. It felt like a fucking desert out here as every bit of the blazing sun shined down on me. It caused my palms to be extra sweaty and I feared that I would lose my grip and somehow slip.

POW! POW!

Half way up the gate, I looked up and spotted at least ten men coming my way. I immediately jumped for the ground but the tail end of my shorts caused me to get stuck.

POW! POW!

A bullet struck me in the shoulder while another one hit me in the hip. I anxiously pulled myself free from the gate, fell to the ground, and then staggered my way to my feet. The feeling in my leg burned as if it had been filled with hot pieces of coal. Running the best I could, I climbed the hill with as much speed as possible, wishing I had gone to the hospital when Rozalyn called. Especially when another bullet grazed by my ear and another one struck me in my left forearm.

"Aghh!" I groaned as I continued to run, determined to make it into the woods, and into safety.

"Get him! Get him!" I could hear the guards yelling as they chased behind me.

Shots continued on all around me but I was able to make it to my duck off spot I created a while ago. I slipped into it and waited until the coast was clear. There was no way they were going to find me in here. I created the hole for a situation such as this one and it was already paying off. I heard the footsteps hustling passed me and could tell they were going crazy not being able to find me. Each one that passed me up could be heard grumbling and cursing to themselves. I just had to wait a few more minutes and then make my way to the hospital.

***

I stumbled into the emergency room of the hospital, feeling at any minute I was going to pass out. I couldn't even tell you how I made it to the hospital alive. I'd been hit so many times and lost so much blood that it wasn't even funny.

I couldn't tell which part of my body hurt the worse or which part would require the most attention. I stumbled my way towards the nurse's desk causing people walking by to jump out of the way. Soon as I made it to the nurse's desk, they began yelling out all kinda of hospital lingo. I used the edge of the desk to hold me up until a few of the staff ran towards me with a gurney. Soon as they laid me across the gurney, they began to cut my clothes open and check my wounds.

Not long after they were sticking me with all kinds of needles and pushing tubes in different places. Soon as I hit the double doors that took me to the trauma area, I passed out and everything went dark.

24: Rozalyn

"Look, I wanna talk to Tae! Get your hands off of me!" I yelled pulling away from one of Tae's guards Nemo.

"Rozalyn, calm down! Tae gave orders to take you to Dallas," Black said.

"Take me to Dallas for what! Who is he to be giving orders? My son is lying up in the hospital, I'm not about to leave him here!" I cried out doing everything to get away from Nemo.

"Some shit about to pop off and Tae wants you safe, just do what they tell you to do. Please?" Black begged.

"What about my son? Zavier? I'm not leaving him here."

"I got him. Don't worry; he'll most likely arrive before you do. Just get in the car and I promise you everything will be good," Black said removing a piece of hair from my face.

I sighed deeply, nodded my head, and helped Tamarion and Zyir into the car. I was so fuckin' pissed I didn't know what to do. Black left the hospital to check on Tamar, and then all of a sudden returned with blood everywhere. He wouldn't elaborate on what was going on but was real detailed on giving orders; orders that I didn't like.

Tae was always into some mess and the shit was always causing problems for the rest of us. I didn't feel as if he had the right to tell what me what to do or where to go being he and I were no longer a couple. I should have a choice on whether I wanted to go to Dallas or not. Who the fuck lives in Dallas anyway? I'm getting so sick of this shit I didn't know what to do. I felt like taking my children, moving out of state, and not telling anyone where we're at.

This has been my life for the past few years and I was growing wearily tired of it. Always running from something, looking over my shoulder, dodging bullets, and all that other non-sense that normal people don't go through. I haven't lived a normal life in years that I honestly couldn't tell you the first thing about it. The time spent without my children was the only time I remember it being quiet with no drama but I wouldn't exactly call that normal. Life without my kids definitely isn't normal.

"Everything will be okay," Xenya said as she looked over her shoulder.

"Yea whatever," I sighed and crossed my arms over my chest.

We were riding in a freaking van with dark tinted windows. I couldn't see anything from inside and that further elevated my nervousness. Messiah was no longer answering his phone and he didn't even attempt to call me back after I pleaded with him to save me from Black and Nemo. I didn't know what that was all about and if I even wanted to know. Messiah seemed to be on some more shit lately, more concerned with what Tamar had going on than me.

The consistency of the questions had me a tad bit suspicious of Messiah's motives. I wanted to mention it to Tamar but didn't know if it was petty. They already didn't like each other and I didn't want any more strife there that didn't need to be.

"Did Black give you any info on Tamar? Did he say where all the blood came from?" I asked and looked over at my boys who seemed just as worried as I did. I realized in order for them to feel safe; then I was gonna have to calm down. I decided to sing a few songs and relax for the remainder of the trip.

****

The time it took to get into Dallas was very drawn out. The city was so damn big that I swore we continue to drive for hours in order to get to where we going. It was so much busier than what I had grown accustomed to in Miami. The entire scene was so urban but also had this laid back feel to it.

When we pulled up into the hood, I almost lost my cool all over again. I couldn't believe that Tamar had us pulled from our comfort zone to go on a long uncomfortable drive, to this rundown place. I won't front and act like I haven't lived in similar environments but I was familiar with them. I didn't know shit about Dallas and damn sure didn't know anyone here.

I picked Zyir up and grabbed Tamarion pulling him close to me. We followed Xenya as she took us to a unit located in the back of the complex. I felt super nervous because she kept looking around as if she was expecting someone to pop out of a bush or something.

"Is everything okay Xenya?" I asked holding tightly to Tamarion's hand.

"Yea sweetie we're good. I just gotta keep an eye out for these cats around here," Xenya stuck her key in the door and pushed it open. She stepped to the side and allowed for us to enter first.

I had to admit that I was truly impressed with the inside way more than the outside. The space was decorated with a little bit of class and much detail. The flat screen TV, an impressive sound system, and immaculate furniture showed that some money and time went into the decorating.

"Um, make yourselves at home. There's the kitchen, the bathroom is through there and to your left, and the last bedroom on the right is where you all can sleep."

I nodded and let out a frustrated sigh. I was so confused and unsure as to what was going on. I called Messiah and Tamar over and over again but couldn't get an answer from either of them. The suspense was killing me very slowly, just waiting to know what has happened to each of the men.

"Black text me and said that your son has arrive safely at Children's hospital and that he will take you to see him in the morning," Xenya said with a smile.

"Okay thank you. Has he said anything concerning Tae?" I asked.

"Last I heard they rushed him to the hospital but--"

"What? Rushed him to the hospital for what? What happened?" I frantically asked.

"I have no idea but you gotta calm down cause you're scaring the kids," Xenya looked at the scared looks on the boys' face and placed her hand over her chest.

I had a feeling that something wasn't right just from when Black came back with all that blood on him. He wasn't talking about sending us out of town before he checked on Tae but suddenly when he came back he was panicky and nervous. I crashed on the couch and both boys came and jumped into my lap. Tamarion pulled hair from my face while Zyir just sat and stared at me.

Xenya offered to make us something to eat while we waited for Black to arrive. I started questioning her again to make conversation and to take my mind off the worry. I found out she was from Africa and has only been living in Dallas for the past eight years. I asked about if she had any sisters or brothers and she seemed to disappear from the entire conversation. I spotted tears gathering in the corners of her eyes and wondered what that was all about.

After Xenya cooked, we sat down, ate, and then made our way to the guest bedroom to rest. I haven't really had a decent amount of rest since Zavier was hospitalized.

"Night, night," Tamarion said followed by his brother Zyir.

"Night, night," I repeated to them.
****

Glass breaking and heavy voices stirred me from my sleep. I jumped from the bed and walked to the bedroom door where I peek my head out the crack. I couldn't see anything but heard clearly the bold voices of someone speaking another language. I tried to stick my head out a little more to get a better view when the door cracked and suddenly the voices stopped.

"No! No! No!"

I heard Xenya shriek out and suddenly heard footsteps coming my way. I pushed the door closed, twisted the lock, and ran over to the boys. Just when I thought about escaping through the window, the bedroom door came crashing down, and two bulky built guys stepped in.

"Please don't hurt my kids," I yelled holding my hands out in front of me.

"Pretty, pretty girl," one of them said. His accent was so thick and rooted that I could barely understand a word that he said.

"Come here!" the other one ordered.

"Please---I didn't do anything!"

The boys had awakened and gathered up together at the top of the bed. I was so fuckin' scared to the point where I almost pissed on myself. The first bulky guy came at me, snatched me by my hair, and pulled me out of the bedroom. *So much for Tamar getting us to safety.* I thought as I was being dragged against my will.

My boys were screaming and hollering for the man to let me go but as soon as we entered into the living room he tossed me next to Xenya. She shook her head no continuously while tears streamed down her dark face like a faucet.

"She doesn't have anything to do with this!" Xenya cried out to a man that held a knife in his hand the same size as the chopper that hung around his body.

"I asked you if anyone else was here and you lied to me Xenya!"

"Because she does not matter! She and the kids needed a place to sleep for the night, I barely know this woman and she barely knows me!" Xenya sniffed.

"Where the fuck is Black?" the goon with the big ass knife ignored Xenya and approached me.

"Bla--Black?" I stuttered. I couldn't believe that Tae entrusted me and his children in the care of a muthafucka that had gorilla looking niggas after him. These dudes looked like they lived on the jungle and hunted animals down for a living. I knew they had to be from the same place as Xenya due to their thick accents.

"The fuck is he at? Tell me now or I'll kill you and those kids back there!" he yelled so ruthlessly that spittle hit me in the face.

"Uncle Enzi, she doesn't even know Black! I promise you she doesn't! Please leave her out of this! I will take you to Black myself but you have to leave her and her kids out of this!" Xenya screamed with force. Her African accent was even more noticeable when she got angry.

The men spoke amongst each other in African dialect for a few moments; the leader suddenly jerked Xenya up from the floor and pulled her out of the apartment with the rest of the goons following behind them. I breathed a sigh of relief not even feeling bad for Xenya, this was her and Black's mess; me and my kids didn't have anything to do with it. I stood up from the floor and got ready to go back to where the kids were in bedroom waiting. I could see the both of them peeking around the corner so I held out both of my arms for them to come to me. Tamarion began to run my way first but he stopped abruptly, his eyes widened, and his mouth dropped open. I looked over my shoulder and spotted one of the African men standing behind me with a gun pointed in my direction. Instantly a tear fell from my eye because I knew there was nothing I could to stop him.

"Enzi said to leave no witnesses," he said.

POW!

25: Tamar

"When I'm not here, I need somebody on him at all times. Do not ever leave him alone, understood?" I said to my guard Nemo.

He nodded his head and moved inside of Zavier's hospital room as I left out. I had just made it to Dallas about an hour ago and came straight here to check on my little man to make sure he was being properly taken care of and properly secured. I didn't know when Donald would send his mob after me but I knew they were coming and I had to be prepared and ready. Dallas was the first place I could think of that I knew Donald wouldn't start and it was also where Black was from. He knew the ins and outs of the city and had plenty of niggas down here ready to go to war for him if needed, but I really hoped that it didn't get to that point. Once I got Rozalyn and the kids comfortable, I would go back to Miami and see Donald and his men head on but for now I had to ensure that everything was good with them. One thing I knew about suckas, they loved to go for your family if they couldn't get to you and that I wasn't going to let happen. I had my moms and sister moved to another location and Taron was a big boy that could handle himself.

"Shit," I groaned as the pain in my wrist began to ache once again.

"You good?" Black asked.

"Shit, throbbing like a muthafucka' but I'll be good," I shook my head.

That bitch Kari turned out to be a real live psycho for real, a fucking head case that I turned out and almost died because of. I knew she had issues but I didn't know the shit ran as deeply as it did. She cut my wrist so damn deep that it sliced an artery that caused me to bleed out quickly and loose consciousness. Had it not been for Rozalyn calling to look for me and her making Black aware that there was a situation that needed tending to; I would've bled to death. I had lost so much blood that the hospital recommended that I stay for a couple of days and heal but I that wasn't happening. Shit was about to go down and I couldn't be laid up recovering from a wound that would eventually heal over time. Long as my ass was able to walk and talk then I didn't see the need in staying. I immediately caught a helicopter to Dallas and began to check on my family; I would worry about the hole in my wrist later.

"So everything is good where Rozalyn and my boys are?" I asked Black as we jumped into his souped up Mercury Marauder.

"Yea, my girl took them back to my place. They are good, you don't have anything to worry about," Black nodded then turned the system up to the max, bumping that old ass 'Many Men' track by 50 cent.

Many men, wish death upon me
Blood in my eye dog and I can't see
I'm tryin' to be what I'm destined to be
And niggas tryin' to take my life away

I put a hole in a nigga for fucking with me
My back on the wall, now you gon' see
Better watch how you talk, when you talk about me
Cause I'll come and take your life away

I sat in silence and listened to every word that 50 cent spit through those speakers. Every word he spoke was nothing but the truth for me but I was ready to cop out and put this shit to rest. The older I got the less and less attractive the game became to me. I'd lost my two best friends, had to kill my own fuckin' father, have my older brother killed and the shit just wasn't stopping. Dmitri was dead and I was being blamed for it, my family is at risk, and I felt like it was me against the world right now. Ordinarily I would've had Keylan and Brandon fighting every battle with me, but I didn't have neither of them and that shit hurt bad as hell. My brother Taron was too damn afraid of catching another case and going back to prison that he kept his hands as clean as possible. It was only me and the outsiders I chose to instill my trust into to fight off the constant haters and enemies I had against me.

"Why the fuck we coming over here?" I asked looking around.

Black laughed, "Chill out nigga I know you ain't scared."

"Hell nah I ain't scared. I'm just saying I know you got money so I know this ain't where you living at right?"

"This is home, it's where I was born and raised," Black said nonchalantly.

"Yea whatever nigga, I wanna see you say that shit when muthafuckas come kicking down your door trying to kill you," I said looking around once again.

"You can't kill a killer."

"Yea whatever," I pulled my pistol from my waistband, and mugged the side of Black like he'd lost his mind. I know for a fact that Rozalyn had to be bugging the fuck out and mad as hell that she was back in the damn hood. I could imagine the Brooklyn accent running real thick right now, ready to light me up the minute she saw me.

"Oh shit!" Black cursed.

I pushed Black out of the way, ran inside of the apartment, and immediately froze upon seeing Tamarion and Zyir laying on top of their mother's bloody body; crying their eyes out.

"Get them!" Black yelled. "Xen! Xenya, where are you?" Black frantically searched the home but came back with a furious look on his face.

I couldn't move or say anything; I just stood and watched as Rozalyn lie dead in a puddle of blood. Every memory, good and bad flashed through my head from the very first time we met, sexual encounters, the fights, the make-ups the break ups; everything.

"Are you following me? Let my arm go!" Rozalyn said as she wiped the tears from her eyes.

"Tae, come on! Don't do this! Fight!

"Tae, I love you! I love you so much! Please don't leave me!" Rozalyn cried after I'd been pumped with a load of bullets.

"You feeling yourself or something? I been gone that long that you forgot who the fuck I was." I said with a handful of Rozalyn's hair.

Memory after memory rushed through my mind, forcing me to remember the reasons why I loved her so much. Pushing me to think about my most vulnerable moments, moments when I felt like the weakest dude alive all because I was in love.

"Tamar! Tamar! Get the boys!" Black handed me Tamarion and Zyir forcing me out of my reverie.

He ran over and scooped Rozalyn up from the floor and ran out of the apartment. I slowly followed behind him, feeling like each step I took was calculated and with force. There was no need to rush and panic because Rozalyn was already dead, it was obvious from all the blood, and the way her body had been limp across the floor. She was lifeless; dead.

26: Messiah

6 weeks later

I've looked everywhere for Rozalyn the moment I was well enough to leave the hospital. Her house hadn't been touched in weeks, her shop had been burned to pieces, and her friend Brian claimed to not know where she was, and she wasn't answering her phone. I missed the hell out of her and really regret not going to her the day she called me. I could only imagine the thoughts that ran through her mind, most likely thinking that I abandoned her. The truth of the matter is I let revenge get in the way of what should've been truly important to me.

I want to see Tae go down so bad that everything I've been doing lately was aimed at that. Revenge coasted my mind so much that it had almost been impossible to think about anything else. All I could seem to think about was getting back at Tae.

Tae has yet to return to his home since the day the ambulance rushed him out of the drive way. I couldn't help but wonder if he and Rozalyn had ran off somewhere, leaving me sitting here looking stupid. I knew the muthafucka' wasn't dead after that chick sliced him up because the shit was all over the news for two weeks straight. She lost her job as lead reporter and sat in jail for a lil' while until someone bailed that ass out. It was reported that Tamar was recovering from his wounds but his location wasn't released.

Finally, I got the location of his brother Taron after following him one night from the club. Don't know why it didn't come to me at first but at least all hope wasn't lost.

"Hey Ron!" I yelled out the moment I stepped out of my car.

He turned around with a pistol aimed in my direction. I jumped back and held my hands up in surrender. "It's me, Sy!"

"Oh shit homey you better say something. Thought you was one of those Italians man," Taron said as he approached me.

We slapped hands and I leaned against the car and watched as Taron looked over his shoulder something he had been doing all night.

"What's this I hear about the Italians?" I asked wondering if they said anything about me.

"Yea, you know we've been at war with them over Dmitri's death---wait you knew about Dmitri right?" Taron asked.

"Nah, I've been out of pocket. Handling some family business." I lied. "So they think someone from your camp did it?"

"They think Tamar did it. They came through and got into a shootout with his security, burned down Rozalyn's shop," Taron sighed. "Hell I got into a shootout with then fools a couple of weeks ago, that's why I'm agg like this."

"Damn, I feel ya. I can't believe Dmitri dead. That was my dude," I said shaking my head as if I was truly hurt. "But aye, I've been trying to get in contact with Rozalyn. It don't look like nobody been at her house and I saw the shop was burned down."

Taron scratched his head and looked around once more. He leaned against my car, whole attitude softening, before he looked back up at me. "Rozalyn was shot in the back and is currently paralyzed from the waist down. They said that it's possible she may walk again but right now she still confined to a damn bed."

Everything seemed to freeze on those last words Taron said, "*Rozalyn was shot in the back and is currently paralyzed from the waist down.*"

I cared about Rozalyn a whole lot although it was never my intention to fall for her, but I did and fell kinda hard. She made me feel special whenever we were together, always listened to me without judgment, and the sex; the sex was amazing. I could only wonder if this happened because I didn't go to see about her that night.

"What hospital can I find her at?" I asked not believing this shit.

"She's not in the hospital anymore."

"Well, where is she? I need to see her man. Where can I find her?"

"Her and my brother going through right now---I don't know if--"

I cut him off, "Aye, I really need to see her. It's not any beef shit fam for real that's my love and I just wanna see her. I gotta see her."

"Alright, alright."

I jotted down the address to where I could find Rozalyn at and thanked Taron for the information. I honestly wasn't trying to go see Rozalyn on no beef shit but I couldn't guarantee that once I saw Tamar that I wouldn't try and put him down. Honestly I was starting to no longer care about getting this nigga money, especially after his security damn near killed me. I had to sit in the hospital hoping that no one ever found me while I healed for the many bullets that I took from them cowards. They tried to kill me over some shit that belonged to me anyway and because of that I wanted to murk Tae with no reservations about it whatsoever.

27: Tamar

I sat back looking over the contents of a thick package I received moments earlier at my doorstep. It was all the information that Black had gathered about Sy while I had been out of town. For the life of me, I couldn't put my finger on why I disliked this dude besides the fact that he was fucking my wife, but seeing this verified that my feelings were just.

I looked over each document carefully, ensuring that I never once misread or misconstrued one word. I wanted everything to be clear so that I knew how to handle this nigga accordingly and when I brought it to Rozalyn. She'd been tripping off not seeing him since her accident and wanted to call and talk to him but I wouldn't allow it. Part of me was jealous that she sought the attention of another man and part of me knew that keeping our location secret was for the best.

I never thought that sending Rozalyn and my kids to Dallas would turn out to be so tragic. All I wanted, all I ever wanted was to protect them. It had been one thing that I've always failed to do as a man and kicked myself repeatedly each time I failed. When I walked in to Black's home and saw Rozalyn lying in a pool of blood; I honestly thought that I'd lost her for good. If Black had not been there, I probably would've lost her being I was so in shock and couldn't function. Him being there and partially saving her life is the only reason I didn't kill that nigga when I found out this shit was on him. Him and his girl Xenya had issues going on with their families and were still going through it. I still used him for work but let that nigga know to stay away from me and my family until his situation was resolved. I didn't want any problems with them damn Africans.

"Hello," I answered my phone before leaving the patio and going back into the house.

"Tae, please talk to me. You know that you are wrong for doing me like this," Kari cried in my ear.

"How many times do I have to tell you to stop calling me?" I asked in a hushed but aggressive tone.

Kari had been calling me almost every day since she's been released from jail. I chose not to press charges against her being I didn't fuck with the police like that. I didn't have time to be up in a court room testifying and going over that day's events. I recommended they put the crazy bitch in the mental ward and put a restraining order on her for me. I knew that if I ever saw her face again, I would kill her with no hesitation. The bitch damn near sent me to early a grave all because of some fatal attraction psycho shit. My brother and Rozalyn both tried to tell me that I should've never led her on but it wasn't like that in the beginning. I honestly got with her thinking I could get over Rozalyn and move on but that will never happen. My heart will always belong to Rozalyn no matter what we went through.

"Tae, what about our baby? How would you like it if I told Rozalyn the only reason you didn't press charges is because I'm pregnant with your child!"

I shook my head, hung up the phone, and headed into the house. I purchased a beautiful beach house down in

Houston, Texas after Rozalyn was released from the hospital. My drama with Donald was still ongoing and I never got a chance to take care of it because I chose to stay with Rozalyn every step of the way and because Zavier also needed intense therapy to get over his injuries. He was half-way through his treatment plan and was already running around with his brothers like nothing happened. Now it was time to work on Rozalyn; she would require the most time and effort.

When the bullet entered her back, it crushed a nerve linked to her spinal cord and caused her to be paralyzed from the waist down. After a few crucial surgeries to repair the nerve, doctors are determined with a lot of hard work that one day she will walk again. I would pay whatever it cost to ensure that she got the best therapist ever to treat her. I hated seeing her confined to a bed and wheel chair not able to move around at her own free will.

"Why you ain't eat that food?" I asked walking into the bedroom.

"I told you I don't like her cooking. She can't cook," Rozalyn said with a frown.

"You just being picky. I told you I can get my mama down here."

"I know I just hate for her to be running all over the country following behind us every time a problem pops off. She was just getting used to Miami the last time I talked to her,"

"She wants to help Roz and besides the kids miss her. I think I'm a bring her down for a few weeks. Her and Lana," I shrugged. "How you feeling this morning?"

"Same way I feel every day. Nothing has changed. As a matter of fact, is it time for me to get my pain meds?"

I flinched at hearing Rozalyn ask for more pain meds. It had only been an hour and a half since her last dose and was nowhere near time for more. I'd seen many of drug addicts in my life and had even been one myself at one point in time. Rozalyn was addicted to the pain killers and the shit was killing me to watch. The doctor warned us that it was possible, but Rozalyn had never shown an addictive type personality so I assumed that it was nothing to worry about.

"Not yet, but look I wanna talk to you about your boy," I said changing the subject.

"My boy?" she questioned raising a brow.

"Yea, that bitch ass nigga Sy you keep asking about."

"Mmgh, what about him? You gonna let me call him?" Rozalyn asked with a roll of her eyes.

"Hell nah, that dude is a fucking psycho and I got paperwork to prove it. You remember when I told you the day Kari sliced my wrist, my security caught somebody trying to jump my fence and break into my crib?" I asked and Rozalyn nodded. "Well it was Messiah. Come to find out, they found a lil' camping ground he had in the back of my house a few days later after they shot that nigga. After that I decided to have him fully investigated and the shit that was found is truly unbelievable."

"Well, what is it?" Rozalyn asked suddenly looking a little concerned.

"First off the nigga name is Marvin Christian and he didn't do no three-four years in the penitentiary like he said. He did all that time in a mental institution for killing his parents and brother."

"What? You gotta be making this shit up. Messiah is not a damn killer or this Marvin dude you're talking about," Rozalyn protested.

"It was the same damn institution that Brandon was in, apparently them niggas was real cool up in that bitch," I shook my head just thinking of all the shit Brandon probably told to Messiah or Marvin or whatever the fuck his name is.

It just didn't make any sense to me, the camp ground that the security found near my house had been there for quite some time. From some of the food wrappers and news paper articles he had been there at least a couple of months before he met Rozalyn which meant he had his reasons for talking to her. I didn't know what this crazy muthafucka' was up to but I was glad to have gotten Rozalyn away from him when I did; even if the circumstances had been crucial.

"Okay, so he was crazy. He's never done anything to hurt me or the kids. What's your point? You really don't wanna see me happy with anybody else but it's okay for you to go around parading with your girlfriend all in my damn face!"

"That muthafuckin' day I got into that accident with the kids Rozalyn, that nigga all of a sudden popped up beating on my window, and asking me why I didn't leave the kids with you. Why the fuck would he be me asking me that? I never thought about it until a week or so ago but I think he's the one that cut my fucking brake line."

Rozalyn shook her head in disbelief as tears slid slowly down her face. I didn't care if it was hurting her to hear or not; I wanted it to hurt. I wanted her to hurt for having the nerve to love another nigga, to request to see or talk to another nigga after I had been the one by her side for the past six weeks. I got my brother still in Miami dodging bullets from the Italian Mob while I'm out here living without so much as having to look over my damn shoulder. I could've been out there fighting my own damn battle and fucking off some of those Italians but the love I had for her wouldn't allow me to just leave like that.

"He was never a drug dealer like he said. It looks like he killed his parents because they wouldn't allow him to sell drugs like his grandfather and his brother Messiah. His brother Messiah was actually the drug dealer that Dmitri assumed Marvin to be. Poor little kid wanted to be just like his grandfather and brother when he grew up that he called himself the next King of Miami." I mocked.

I was so impressed with the work that Black had done in getting the information on Marvin Christian who was originally from the Virgin Island. I held his entire therapy record in my hands, from the very first day he entered into the facility up until the last day he was released. This muthafucka' was crazy as fuck and I wondered how in the hell he was able to get out and be free with that mind of his. Damn, I know I killed my damn pops but it was for good damn reason; this fool killed his whole damn family all because he wanted to sale dope and live up to some dream of running shit and being a fuckin' king. It pissed me off thinking about how this fool had been in my wife's presence all this time, had been around my kids, even around me, but he was still breathing. Although, I didn't have the proof needed, I know he cut my brake line just like I know that he killed Dmitri. All of it seemed like too much of a coincidence to not be so. Before Dmitri brought this nigga around me things were cool, there were the everyday problems that came with the game but nothing major. All of a sudden he pops up and drugs are missing and I'm being blamed for it, my brakes are cut and me and my kids are almost killed and now that I really think about it---

"Oh shit! Look, I'm about to get my moms down here for real to come and look after you. I need to take a trip to Miami to handle some muthafuckin' business!" I got up from the chair I was sitting in and stormed out of the room.

This muthafucka was most likely responsible for putting that homemade ass bomb under my car. Who else could've done it? I didn't have beef like that with anyone to make them wanna blow me the hell up. I was about to be on a flight out to Miami within the next few days; this fool Sy had me fucked up. His records may claim he's crazy but he ain't seen shit yet.

28: Rozalyn

Everything on the table, including me went crashing to the floor. This was the second time in the past couple of weeks that I tried to get out of bed without the help of Tamar or the nurse. Doctors said that I wasn't completely paralyzed and that with a lot of work I would one day be able to walk again. My legs felt like they were worth a good three hundred pounds each which meant to me that if I could feel that weight then I could walk. Each time I tried, I fell flat on my ass, frustrating my anger, and making a damn fool of myself. I knew as soon as Tamar came in here and saw me lying helplessly on this floor he was gonna fuss at me for doing this bullshit again. The fall wasn't a pretty one either, it ignited further pain, and yes made me want them damn pain meds that for some reason he didn't like for me to have.

No doubt, I appreciated Tamar being here for me, sticking by my side and helping me through all of this; I really did. He could've put me in the rehabilitation center at the suggestion of the doctors, left me there until I recovered, and only visited me on the weekends; but he didn't. He was deeply involved in my care, made sure he took the directions of the doctors seriously, and was always around when it was time for my therapy. I loved Tamar for everything that he was doing at this present time but it still didn't change the fact that all this happened because of him. He was the one that had me pulled out of Miami and taken to his worker's house in Dallas. I didn't care if he wasn't aware of problems that Black and Xenya had; he should've known. He should've made sure he was aware of where he was sending his wife and kids. And where the fuck was Xenya and Black now after I got caught up in their bullshit. Now because of all that, I'm forced to sit up in bed for twelve to thirteen hours of the day, pissing in a damn bag and shitting in a fucking pan. I'm a grown ass woman that has to be wiped like a fucking baby every day.

I hated to be mean to Tamar and yes I purposefully asked for Messiah on a daily basis just to piss him off. I wanted him to hate me as much as I hated him right now, hoping that maybe he would conjure up enough nerve to kill me, or just allow me to take enough pills to kill my damn self. I made sure I talked to him crazy every day, never replied to him when he told me he loved me; rejected his kisses, his hugs, and everything hoping that he would stop loving me. I hated to see him loving me so much when I hated him so badly right now. It was sickening to see that he still cared for my cripple ass and for some twisted reason wanted to work on our marriage. I just didn't get his way of thinking at all and I honestly don't believe that I will ever get it.

"Shit Rozalyn!" Tamar ran into the room, raced over to me, and gently lifted me off of the floor

During the fall, I'd ended bringing my piss bag along with me and was now covered in pee. I began to cry as Tamar placed me back in the bed, especially after I spotted the frown that appeared on his face when he caught a whiff of my urine.

"I'm useless. Just let me die Tae! Just let me die!" I cried.

"Come on man, don't start that shit. I told you I'm here for you. We gonna get through this," Tamar said. "I'm finna clean this up and then I'm a put you in the tub. Don't try to move again. A'ight. Hold up."

"Mama okay?" Tamarion asked.

I looked up and spotted Tamarion standing in the doorway with a toy truck in his hand and a sad look on his face. The boys didn't understand what was going on with me, why mommy was always in bed, why she never cooked for them anymore, or came to play with them. All the things that I've grown accustomed to since getting the boys back in my life had been taken away all over again and that hurt me more than anything in this whole world. Seeing them outside building sand castles on the beach, or even trying to get close enough to water without me; crushed me deeply. I so bad wanted to give up, attempt suicide once again, and hopefully succeed this time.

"Yea mama okay. Go back and play with your brothers, I'll be in there in a minute," Tamar said to him.

Tamarion didn't do as his father asked him to do but instead stood by and looked on curiously. I couldn't help but crack a smile at him as he nosily looked on trying to figure out just what his father was doing on the floor.

"Mama is okay," I said weakly.

"Okay mama!" he yelled excitedly and took off running.

Soon as Tamar cleaned up the mess I'd made, he went into the bathroom to draw me some water for a bath. The stench of the piss all over me was starting to make me sick to my stomach and I couldn't wait to get out of the dampened clothes.

Soon as my body hit the hot water I felt as if I weighed a ton, the water seemed to make me feel heavier than ever, as if the water was seeping through my pores and filling me up.

"My mama will be here in a couple of days and as soon as she gets here I'm flying out so I can handle that business," Tamar said as he rubbed my back with a sponge.

"What business is that? Messiah—or Marvin?" I inquired.

"Rozalyn you don't have to believe me but that nigga started talking to you to get at me for whatever reason. I ain't never met Me--Messiah a day in my life until Dmitri introduced me to him but for some reason this dude got it out for me. I need to handle that before he handles me. I know for a fact he's responsible for all the shit that's been happening. He killed Dmitri and got them fucking Italians after me man," Tamar said as his voice cracked.

I looked over at Tamar and noticed his eyes began to water in the corners. He wouldn't admit it but I knew better than anyone how much Tamar loved Dmitri and how much Dmitri loved him. I knew that his death hit him hard and if Messiah was truly responsible for Dmitri's death then maybe I was mad at the wrong person. The main reason I tried to get out of the bed on my own this time was because I wanted to get to those papers to see if just what Tamar had said about Messiah being psycho was true. I couldn't believe that I was such a bad judge in character that I couldn't pick out one decent male. Every nigga that I've ever been with intimately was fuckin' bananas and that shit just didn't sit well with me.

"You think he really did it Tae? You think he killed Dmitri like that?" I asked for reassurance.

"I'm not one-hundred percent but I know I didn't do it Rozalyn," Tamar said as he began to rinse the soap of me.

"I know that you didn't do it. I knew that when I first heard that rumor but—I just don't wanna believe that I put my life at risk like that. Put my kids' lives at risk. I'm such a bad judge of character and what's so crazy is you told me a while back that I didn't know who Messiah was and that I was going to find out. I should've listened to you. If he cut your brake lines, I want him dead. My kids could've died that fuckin' day," I said suddenly feeling a sense of rage.

"Oh I'm a take care of that. Don't you even worry about that."

I looked into Tamar's face, stared him in his eyes, and gently smiled at him, "I'm sorry."

"You ain't gotta apologize Rozalyn. I know that you blame me and truthfully it is my fault but that's not why I'm here for you. I'm not here because I feel guilty, I'm here because I love you and I wanna see to it that you get better."

I sighed, "Do you honestly think that I will walk again?"

"Yea, I know that you will walk again. You just gotta work at it, don't worry I'm a help you," Tamar leaned in and kissed me on the cheek. I turned my head towards him and kissed him on the lips. We stared into each other's eyes, not saying a word, but just allowing our thoughts consume the space that was between us. I took it upon myself to kiss him again, pulled his bottom lip into my mouth and sucked it; savoring the taste of my husband.

"Love you Roz."

"I love you too Tamar. I never stopped," I admitted.

29: Tamar

Once my moms was around, I showed her around the house and prepped her on what to expect with Rozalyn. The live-in nurse I hired was supposed to be the nanny as well. Lately she has been spending more time caring for the boys than she has for Rozalyn being she wasn't that good of a cook and they just couldn't get along. My mom being here would allow me to be able to breathe while I was gone because I knew she would take good care of Roz and the kids. I also decided to give the nurse a few days off to go home and visit family to see if Rozalyn's attitude would change without the nurse being around. If it did, then I knew it would be best for me to hire someone new.

A few days ago, I got in contact with Black to let him know what my suspicions were about Marvin aka Messiah. I wanted to see if he could help me prove that this nigga had been trying to kill me and that he was responsible for Dmitri's death. The inkling at my heart told me that I was right about it all and all I needed was proof to get them Italians to go the fuck away. Donald should know that I'm not the one that killed his damn son but I guess he needed someone to blame for his loss. He wanted me to come to him and confess to some bullshit that I didn't do and that wasn't about to happen.

"Aye, I'm about to leave. You good?" I asked as I stepped into Rozalyn's room.

She nodded her head but didn't say anything. From the look on her face, I could tell that something was bothering her so I dropped my bags and went over to the bed. I leaned down and kissed her on the lips, the cheek, and then on the forehead.

"What's wrong?" I asked.

"I tried to get out of bed again last night while everybody was sleep," Rozalyn said.

"What? Why? You gotta stop doing that shit before you really hurt yourself."

"I was able to do this time Tae. I put myself in the wheelchair, I did it on my own this time," Rozalyn said excitedly. She was so excited that I couldn't even be mad at her. It was good to see that she was trying but she could seriously hurt herself if she fell the wrong way and I would've preferred she tried when someone else was around to assist her.

"How did you get back in the bed?" I asked looking around seeing that everything was in place.

"I did that too. I'm getting stronger everyday," she smiled. "I needed to see those papers that you left over there. I believed you but I just had to see for myself that Messiah was this Marvin like you were saying he was. I can not believe that I spent all that time with someone who is as looney as he is."

"I think we both was fucking with some nut cases ma," I laughed.

"You still haven't heard from Kari?" Rozalyn asked.

"Nah, she's not gonna call me. She doesn't want me pressing charges against her so she knows to leave me the fuck alone," I lied. I placed another kiss on Rozalyn's lips and headed out of the room, picking my bags up along the way. "See you later, a'ight?"

"See you later."

***

Once I made it to Miami, my brother Taron and Black were at the house waiting for me to arrive. Walking in, I noticed the somber looks on each of their faces and immediately felt like something was wrong.

"Fuck wrong with ya'll?" I asked dropping my bags to the ground.

"You want the bad news or the good news first?" Black asked.

"What's the good news cause the way ya'll looking I got a feeling I really ain't gonna sit well with that bad news."

"I found the video of Messiah or this Marvin dude killing Dmitri. Nigga had the nerve to still have the shit like he was keeping it for a souvenir or some shit. And on top of that I found a book of everything he'd planned to take care of in the next twelve months. Blowing up your car had been his first attempt at killing you. He said that since he failed at that, then he was going to torture you by fucking your wife, watching you suffer, taking your status, and then killing you."

I chuckled, "Fucking Looney Tune ass nigga. Fuck him, where the fuck is he so I can handle this nigga ASAP? Muthafucka' tried to kill me and my fuckin' shorties and he think I wasn't gonna figure that shit out! I want that nigga so bad I can fuckin' taste his blood in my mouth!"

"Aye, that's the bad news," Black said looking over at Taron.

Taron took a deep breath, ran his hands across his face, and then crashed on the couch, "I gave that nigga the address to where ya'll were at."

"What the fuck? You did what?" I bellowed.

"Man I didn't know he was on some bullshit like this. He came to my crib and told me he really wanted to see Rozalyn. He didn't even know what happened to her," Taron said shaking his head.

"What the fuck you mean he came to your crib? You invited that nigga to your house Taron?"

"Nah, he just showed up. I thought he was one of those Italians but once I saw it was him, we sat and chopped it up and he said he wasn't on no beef shit. He said that he really wanted to see Rozalyn, and that he loved her."

"Ron, you gotta be one of the dumbest niggas I know. How the fuck do this nigga even know where you stay? Did you even think of that? Why the hell would you give this nigga the address to where I'm keeping my wife and kids? I've been telling you since day one that something wasn't right about that muthafucka' and you send him to me! I swear to God if you wasn't my brother I would murk your dumb ass right now!" I pulled out my cell phone and dialed my moms' number to see if everything was okay. This shit was just unfuckinbelievable, unacceptable, and just flat out crazy. My brother had to be the dumbest cat on the planet right now for that mess he did for real.

"I'm sorry bro! I wasn't thinking straight. I thought it would've been cool," Taron said.

"How long ago was this Taron? When did you give him the address?" I asked.

"A couple of days ago," he answered.

"I already sent a couple of people down there Tae so everything should be good," Black said.

"This nigga could've already been at the house, watching and waiting on me to slip up so he can strike! I gotta go---gotta get to the airport and back to Houston immediately," I grabbed my bags and turned to walk out of the door with Black following behind me.

"I appreciate you still fucking with me Tae. Money is tight right now and every lil' thing you throw my way helps man no doubt," Black said as he ran to keep up with me.

"Yea, yea---take me to the airport," I said not giving a fuck about none of that shit he was saying.

"Okay, get in!"

The whole ride to the airport, Black kept apologizing over and over about what happened to Rozalyn and how he was working to handle the niggas that did the shit to her. I only nodded my head and half-way listened to what he had to say being my head was so consumed with thoughts of the wife and kids. I hoped to God that Messiah wasn't already there and that the security Black sent would arrive soon. I couldn't take it if something else happened to Rozalyn, or even to my damn kids.

I breathed a sigh of relief when my phone rung and the caller ID showed Rozalyn's name. I'd called her several times back to back and didn't receive an answer, "Hello."

"Daddy!" Tamarion said into the phone.

"Marion, what's up man? Where your mama at? Go take the phone to your mama."

"Mama's crying and granny is sick," he said.

"What you mean mama is crying and granny is sick? Where is mama at?" I asked. My heart beat rapidly in my chest thinking of all the things that could've been meant by what my son just said. "Is somebody hurting your mama? Did somebody hurt granny?"

"Yes and we scared daddy. Can you come home?"

"I'm on my way home son. Everything gonna be okay. I want you and your brothers to hide in the closet and keep quiet until I get there, okay?"

"Okay daddy bye!" he said before the phone went dead.

A single tear fell from my eye as fear and frustration took over. I've never been so fucking scared in my damn life, scared of what happened to my mama, to Rozalyn, and what would happen to my kids. I knew that it would take me forever to get to Houston and that bothered more than anything. Knowing that while I was going through the airport trying to book a plane, my family was suffering at the hands of lunatic.

"I should've put two in Ron's head for this shit," I said wiping tears away with the back of my hand.

"He's there huh?" Black asked.

"I have a feeling that he is. How along go did you send the security down there?"

"A couple of hours ago soon as Taron told me. I tried to get you but I guess you were already on the plane and on the way here."

"Muthafuckin' Sy, Marvin aka Messiah. That nigga got several bullets with his name on it," I sighed.

30: Messiah

"Why the fuck are you being like this?" I asked Rozalyn but once again she wouldn't answer me. She only stared at me as if the bullet affected her speech as much as it affected her legs. Soon as Taron gave me the information on where to find Rozalyn, I drove around for a few hours before deciding to just drive down here to Houston. The moment I pulled up to the house, I immediately felt a twinge of jealously cross over me causing me to be sick to my stomach. It was amazing how this nigga could leave a mini-mansion in Miami and then come to Houston and live in a house sitting on the beach coast like people just did this shit every day.

I sat for two days watching in agony, as Tamar played on the beach with the boys, chilling and just having a good ol' time like he didn't have a care in the world. This is the kind of life I wanted ever since I was a kid, the kind of life that my grandfather and brother tried to provide for us but failed to do once they were both murdered. The kind of life that I planned to make for myself and whatever family I had until I was stopped and forced to do time. This life was stolen from me by Tamar and I wanted it back, however I had to get it; I was gonna get it.

"Rozalyn, talk to me! Why are you being like this with me? I haven't done anything wrong, what have I done to you?" I questioned.

"You killed your parents Marvin?" Rozalyn stunning me when she finally opened her mouth.

"What---how did---who told you that?" I stuttered. "Why are you calling me Marvin?"

"And your brother? Mes—Marvin, you told me you went to jail for drugs. Why did you lie to me?"

"I did go to jail for drugs! You don't know nothing about me or what I've been through! Who told you that bullshit? Your husband told you that? He just wants to take everything away from me!" I yelled swiping the plate of food that sat on a tray in front of Rozalyn to the floor.

"You're crazy! The fuck away from me!" Rozalyn said looking at me with fear in her eyes.

"I'm not crazy Rozalyn. I'm not crazy! Tell you just like I told my mama and them doctors! I'm not crazy so don't fuckin' call me that again!"

I leaned in and kissed Rozalyn on her lips but she turned her head away from me, brought her hand up, and knocked me upside of my head. I looked at her as if she had lost her mind and tried to kiss her again. She'd never turned away from me before so I didn't understand what her problem was now.

"Rozalyn, why are you turning away from me? I love you baby," I said and kissed her once more.

"Messiah, Marvin whoever the fuck you are get away from me! You don't love me because if you did you would have never cut Tamar's brake line! You could've killed my damn kids!"

"He was the only one that was supposed to be in the car! I tried to get him to leave the kids with you!" I yelled.

"You almost killed Zavier, Messiah. You almost killed him!"

I began to pace the floor back and forth, wondering how in the hell did Rozalyn find all of this out. I knew it was possible that Tamar would find out about me cutting his brake line but damn how did she know that I killed my parents and my brother. My record was supposed to be sealed after I left that place and no one was supposed to be able to find out what I had done.

"I just want my money and I want my crown. That's it!" I bellowed and walked out of the room. I stepped over the old lady that I knocked over the head when I first came into the house and made my way to the master bedroom to search for anything of value. Tamar had to have some money around here somewhere. I pulled out dresser drawers, tossed clothes everywhere, flipped the mattresses over, and then went to search the closet. If I found a little bit of money then I could start my own drug organization and quickly take Miami back over.

I came across a wad of money wrapped in a rubber band and then frowned seeing that it was only a couple of thousand dollars. Stuffing it in my pocket, I left out of the master bedroom and went into the kid's room to search all over again. I did their room the same way and when I found nothing, I went into the closet, and began to search there. I moved shoes and toys out of the way and froze when I came across something solid and warm. I pulled at it and slid it from underneath its hiding place seeing that it was one of Rozalyn's twins. He looked at me with tears filling his eyes, and then back at his two brothers who were now suddenly standing behind him.

"Who are ya'll hiding from?" I asked. The twin pointed into my chest and then looked back at his brothers once more.

BLAM!

"Okay, go back into your hiding place. I'm going to close the door and go check on your mama okay?" I pushed the twin back and stood up to leave out of the closet. I didn't have an interest in hurting the children unless I was left with no other choice. I went back into the room where Rozalyn was and noticed that she was no longer in the bed. "How the fuck did she get out of the bed?"

I looked around the room, under the bed, checked the closet but didn't find Rozalyn at all. She was supposed to be paralyzed from the waist down so I couldn't understand where she could've gone. I left out of the room and began to search the house frantically knowing that she couldn't have gotten that far.

"Rozalyn, where the fuck are you? Come on Rozalyn, where are you? I didn't come here to hurt you! I need my money and I need to reclaim my crown! I will always be king of Miami! Do you hear me? Tamar ain't shit! My family started this shit for him, if it wasn't for my grandfather and my brother paving the way for me then Miami wouldn't be shit. I made it possible for Tamar to make money out here and he owes me for that shit! I am the fuckin' king and he needs to know that because of me all of this possible. He owes me!"

BLAM!

I hurriedly turned around and ran in the direction of where the noise had come from knowing that it had to be Rozalyn. I cautiously walked into the master bedroom, looked around but still didn't see her anywhere. I took light steps keeping my ears open, listening for more noise so I would be able to detect exactly where she is the moment she moved again.

"Roza—"

POW! POW!

Two bullets stung me right in the middle of the back; I turned around to see Rozalyn gripping the handle of a nine millimeter tightly while pointing it in my direction. I moved a couple of steps towards her but was stopped when she started firing again.

POW! POW! POW! POW!

31: Rozalyn

I shook violently on the bedroom floor, gripping the gun, and still pointing it in Messiah's direction. I could tell that he wasn't dead yet because his chest rose and fell rapidly and his leg was moving up and down against the floor. I didn't know if he planned on hurting me or the kids but I didn't want to take a chance especially not after hearing what he did to his family. I used my upper body's strength to slide across the floor to where Messiah was laying at with his eyes open staring into space.

I bypassed him and kept moving until I was in the hallway where I spotted Cheryl laying across the floor. My body became weaker but I kept fighting until I was able to get to her and see if she was okay. Once I made it over to her, I reached in and checked for a pulse and noted that she was still breathing but knocked out cold.

"Tamarion! Boys!"I yelled out and began to shake Cheryl. "Zavier, Zyir! Tamarion!"

Tamarion came running around the corner full speed with his brothers right behind him. I could tell that they'd been crying from the dried up tears on their little faces. I hated that they had to go through all this and regretfully wished that I could take everything so violent and bad that they have seen back. I held my hands out and each one of them came running over to me, hugging me, and kissing me all over. I laughed and was so thankful that I was able to get control of that situation before it got out of hand.

"Tamarion, where is the phone? Can you go get me the phone?" I asked him.

Tamarion nodded his head and took off running into his bedroom and I began to shake Cheryl again attempting to awaken her. She moved slightly but never once opened her eyes to look up at me. I waited until Tamarion came back with the phone and once he did, I dialed 911 to call for help for Cheryl. I didn't give a damn about Messiah and I hoped that by time they arrived that he had completely passed on and went to hell where he belonged.

***

It was well into the night when Tamar arrived back in Houston to the beach house. Police, along with crime scene investigators, and paramedics, and other staff walked up and through the house for hours trying to figure what had happened here. I explained to them that Messiah had broken into the house, assaulted Cheryl, and then came after me. They seemed to get lost on how I was able to get out of the bed and shoot Messiah down but I made them aware that I was capable of getting out and into my wheel chair when I needed to. They seemed to be okay with my story after I told it to them the same way three times over and then especially after I told them about how he did time in the crazy house and his name wasn't really Messiah. They said that they will be in touch with me if they needed more information. I watched helplessly as they went through taking pictures of everything, polishing the entire place for fingerprints, and looking around at papers that were sitting out in the open.

"I'm so sorry. So, so sorry," Tamar said to me and to his mom.

"You don't have to keep apologizing Tamar, it's cool. We're all okay," I said.

"Ma, you good? You okay?" Tamar asked looking over his mom.

"Tamar, we're fine. They checked me out and said I just have a bump on my head. I'm okay baby, stop worrying."

"Damn, I just can't believe this shit," Tamar stood up to his feet and began to pace the floor. Some inaudible words rolled off his tongue and his arms swung back and forth, signaling that he was mad.

"Can you please just help me to the bed? I'm tired and just wanna rest,' I said.

Tamar nodded his head and came over to me, scooping me up from the sofa and taking me into my bedroom. I could understand that he was mad because he wasn't here when Messiah came but there was nothing that could be done about it. I killed Messiah and thankfully no one else was hurt in the process. It was time for us to forget about what happened and just move the hell on, focus on our children, and just maybe focus on us having a marriage. Tamar wanted us to get back together and work through our marital problems but I was still on the fence about that. No matter if Messiah was crazy or not he still treated me better than Tamar has ever treated me and I will never forget him for that. Personally I just felt like we both needed to work on ourselves before we tried to work things out and be together again.

"How you feel?" Tamar asked once he put me into bed.

"I'm okay. I'm just really, really tired," I sighed.

"I mean how do you feel knowing that you just killed someone? That's not something that you can do and expect to sleep well at night."

"I don't feel anything Tamar besides the excruciating pain that's in my neck and shoulders right now," I frowned.

"A'ight, let me figure out where Dalia left your pain meds at and I'll be back," Tamar nodded and walked away.

When Tamar returned with my pain meds, we sat and talked for a little while until he ended up falling asleep in a chair that sat alongside of my bed. I watched him as he slept and suddenly wondered if I told him the truth about the twins would he still feel the same way about them or even about me. I knew that if I ever came out and told him the truth about the one simple mistake that I made back before I got pregnant with the twins he would definitely try to kill me again.

32: Tamar

2 months later

"It's nice but I really don't think you need to leave Miami," Taron said looking around the property that I'd just purchased in Dallas.

"Who said I was leaving Miami? I got a house here, a beach house in Houston, and a house in Miami. I'm keeping all of them bro," I said with a smirk.

"Oh yea I forgot you balling like that. Everybody ain't able," Taron laughed.

"Damn right everybody ain't able. I worked hard to be able to do this," I said once we got into the car. "So, how is Keymani and Toya doing man? I need to get around to meeting my niece."

"Yea you do. She is everything in the world to me right now. I never knew that being a father would feel so great."

"Yea, it's a good feeling. You know the boys are everything to me man and that will never change even though the twins aren't mine."

"Hey, I've been meaning to tell you that J.B. stopped through the club last weekend looking for Rozalyn. Said he's been trying to get in contact with her but the number he got isn't working and I ain't wanna disturb ya'll with it."

"J.B.? Fuck is he looking for Rozalyn for?" I asked in confusion.

"He never sad why, he said that he really needed to get in contact with her."

J.B. is one of my very loyal clients that I've been dealing with since my Atlanta days. He's always copped big weight from me, giving me plenty of money but I didn't understand why he wanted to speak with Rozalyn and not me. He's maybe only met her one time which was at the damn meet and greet party I did when I first moved to Miami a long damn time ago.

"Let me call this nigga and find out. He ain't got no business looking for my wife. I don't understand that shit," I pulled out my cell phone and scrolled through my contacts until I came across J.B.'s phone number.

"Aye, what's up bro?" J.B. said the moment he picked up the phone.

"Headed back to the crib mane, what's going on? My bruh telling me you came through looking for my wife. What's good?" I asked getting right to the point.

"Shit she contacted me a few weeks ago but a nigga was doing time on that lil' ol' assault case I was telling you about. I just came home---"

"J.B., I don't give a fuck about none of that. Why the fuck are you looking for my wife?"

"Nigga, she text me and asked me to come give blood for her shorty. That's why the fuck I'm looking for her."

"What the fuck nigga? You must be ready to lose your muthafuckin' life, I know like hell you ain't fuck my bitch J.B.?"

"Yo, this shit happened over two damn years ago bro. You threatening my life behind that trifling ass bitch nigga?

Word, I just really wanna find out what she talking about with lil' man. Tell the hoe to hit me up!"

The line clicked in my ear signaling that J.B. had hung up the phone. I shook my head back and forth not believing that this bitch stepped out on me with one of my fuckin' clients. It was bad enough she fucked my boy, but now I find out she slept with a client too. These past few months I've been catering to her every need, doing everything in power to ensure that she had the best treatment possible. If it wasn't for that, her ass would be sitting in a fucking rehabilitation center probably still struggling to get out of bed. I put my all into trying to build and repair what we had and now I find this shit out. Every fuckin' time I think that we can work it out and be a fuckin' family something always pops up and gets in the damn way.

"What should I do bruh? It seems like every time I try to make it work, drama always gets in the middle and pulls us apart."

"What the fuck was that all about?" Taron asked.

"Rozalyn apparently text this nigga asking him to give blood to Zavier. The only reason why she would be texting him that is if she suspects that he may be the father which means they fucked."

"Damn man I don't know what to tell you. Is she sleeping with anybody else now?" Taron asked.

"Hell if I know. I thought I knew Rozalyn but it's obvious, I don't know shit."

"I'm saying though, it was the past. Even if she did fuck around on you and slept with J.B. and whoever else the shit was in the past. How many bitches did you sleep with while ya'll were together and still sleeping with now? And don't forget you still got Kari hiding in the back waiting to pop that baby out."

I sighed deeply thinking about what Taron just said to me. He was actually making good sense for once in his damn life. It was true that I have been sleeping with other chicks but that was only because I refused to call Kari's crazy ass up and Rozalyn still wasn't in a position to have sex. She was now walking with the use of a cane but wasn't able to be on her feet for long periods of a time. Any progress was better than no progress but I knew that we still had a long ways to go before she was back to her normal self again. Since we've been in Houston, I've had Rozalyn's house put up for sale and even stopped the reconstruction on her beauty shop. It will be a while before she would be able to be on her own again and I didn't want her worrying about her property in Miami.

It took us about three hours to drive from Dallas to Houston and on the way there I decided that I wasn't going to allow things done in the past affect my relationship with Rozalyn. I was going to confront her about J.B. and let her know that I knew what she'd done but I was gonna do my best to not let it affect me. I wasn't a saint either and had been doing plenty of wrong myself lately.

"Damn, I love it out here. I would stay out here forever if I was you," Taron said looking around.

"Hell nah, it's cool for the spring and summer but I know once the winter comes we not gonna wanna be here," I said sticking the key in the hole and unlocking it and going into the house.

Taron took comfort on the living room sofa while I went to search for Rozalyn. She had some explaining to do and we really needed to talk. I wanted to see where her head was at and to see if she wanted this relationship or not. I knew before she didn't and was on the fence about it but lately she'd warmed up to the idea and I wanted to see just what was going through her mind.

"What's up?" I asked as I sat on the bed next to Rozalyn

"Nothin', I just put the boys to sleep and was gonna try and get me a nap in. Did you take care of things in Dallas?" she asked.

"Yea but look I need to know about you and this J.B. situation?" I asked calmly.

Rozalyn sat up in the bed and bit on her lip but she didn't say anything. She looked all over the place but never once did she make eye contact with me.

"Just tell me the truth; I wanna know if it's true. Did you sleep with him and is it possible that the twins are his?"

She nodded her head yes, "Umm, a couple of times he came down to Miami to do business with you and somehow we just hooked up. It was when we were having all those problems after I found out about Danesha and then when you caught me with Brandon. It only happened a couple of times and I never contacted him again after I knew that my marriage was really what I wanted. He tried to see me a few times afterwards but I let him know that I had made a mistake. I didn't ever talk him again for a while until Zavier's accident."

I nodded my head and respected the fact that she was being honest with me. I burned up on the inside but it wasn't like I was innocent and doing right my damn self.

"What do you wanna do Rozalyn? Do you wanna be with me or not?"

"Yes and I think that the counseling sessions we were supposed to take to get divorced we should take to stay together. We have a lot of issues that need to be worked on," Rozalyn said softly.

"Yea we do have a lot of issues that's for sure," I said.

"I'm sorry, I know I was wrong but like I said before I was on a path of destruction and didn't care about anything else."

Rozalyn moved over to me slowly and kissed me on my neck before moving around and kissing me on my lips. She gently pushed me back on the bed and climbed on top of me.

"Damn, what you doing? You buggin' right now," I said wondering where all this was coming from.

"Doctor said that I am getting stronger and stronger each day and said that I should be able to get rid of my cane and be running in another month."

Rozalyn leaned down and kissed my lips, reaching below, and unzipping my pants. She pulled my dick from my boxers, and gently massaged it through the tips of her fingers.

"You sure it's okay for you to do this?" I asked.

"Yes, the doctor said that it was okay and that it would be good for my muscles. I think that you should get on top though," Rozalyn said as she lay back onto the bed.

I got up and pulled my pants all the way off and then climbed in between Rozalyn's legs. Her pussy was already dripping wet from anticipation, and I slowly slid my dick inside, flinching at the grasp of her muscles squeezing tightly onto my dick.

"I'm sorry Tae. Please forgive me. I'm so sorry," Rozalyn cried as I stroked her wetness.

"We're gonna get our shit together. We got to. I can't take seeing you with nobody else," I said as I stroked her deeply.

***

I was not expecting at all to come home and receive sex from Rozalyn but boy was I glad I did. I had gotten up out of the bed to get us a couple of bottles of water so that we could get back to it. Rozalyn said that she was able to go a couple of more rounds and I was for damn sure going to give her a couple of more. I hadn't showed up to any of the counseling sessions at all when the judge ordered me to because I didn't want to lose my wife but if I needed to show up to keep her then I would. I couldn't take her being with anyone else and was for certain that if I saw her with another dude I would probably flip out and go crazy just like that fool Messiah.

"Tae, bring me a bottle of water," Taron yelled.

POW!

I jumped at the sound of a gun going off in the other room and immediately dropped the bottles to the floor to see what was going on. Once I tried to reach for my gun that I had tucked away in the kitchen, a cold piece of steel was being pressed into the side of my head.

"I'm tired of being ignored by you Tae," Kari's voice shook as she spoke.

"Kari, what the fuck are you doing here?" I asked calmly.

"I wanna know why you keep ignoring me. What have I done that was so bad that you can't talk to me and even acknowledge that we have a baby on the way."

"Did you shoot my brother Kari? Let me get him some help,"

"I don't give a fuck about your brother Tae! You and I need to talk about what we're going to do about our child!"

"Oh my God, Tae!" Rozalyn yelled as she stood a few feet away. Her eyes went from me, to Kari, and then around the corner where I assumed Taron was.

"Bitch, I fuckin' hate you! This is your fuckin' fault!" Kari yelled.

Kari knocked me in the head with the butt of the gun; the blow sent me to flying to the marbled kitchen floor. Kari stepped over me and stormed into Rozalyn's direction. She knocked her over and ended up falling on the floor along with her where she started punching her repeatedly in the face. Rozalyn reached up and hit Kari a few times until she rolled off of her onto her back. Rozalyn grabbed at her cane, stood up to her feet, and was about to hit Kari with the cane until she noticed her swollen abdomen.

"Yes, I'm pregnant with his child bitch! I'm not going anywhere! I'm going to remain in the picture!" Kari yelled as she climbed to her feet, retrieving the gun from the floor.

I shook off the dizziness I was feeling, rolled over onto my stomach, and got up on my feet. I ran over to the two of them just as they began to fight again. They started punching each other back and forth, Kari having the advantage because of the gun. Just as I went to grab the gun out of Kari's hand, she stepped back and began firing.

"Roz, watch out!" I yelled.

POW! POW! POW!

To be continued.

COMING 2013 THE DRAMA OF THE ROZALYN SERIES
CONTINUES

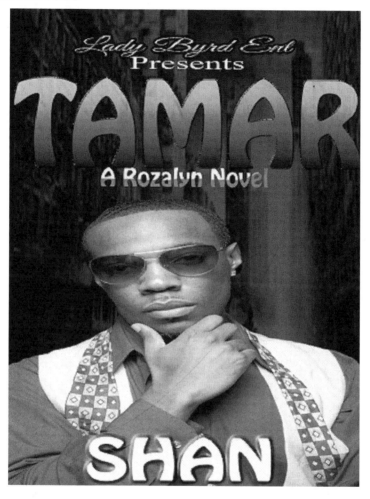

Check out other books by Shan available on Barnes and Noble and Amazon

Reigning Starr
When it Rains it Pours

www.facebook.com/Author.shan

Join my Fan Page on Facebook

https://www.facebook.com/groups/myss.shan/

Follow me on twitter

@myss_Shan

About the Author

Shantoinette Richardson but known as Shan, a Louisiana native but raised in Dallas, Texas. She is the author of the Urban Fiction series Rozalyn and Reigning Starr. She also holds a short story in an anthology titled: When it Rains it Pours.

Writing started off to Shan as just something to do to suppress the pain and hurt she felt growing up as a child to a mother that was addicted to crack and a father who seemed to move on with his life with a new family.

At just 15 years old Shan gave birth to her first child; a baby boy. Being a teen mom didn't stop Shan from achieving her goals. She graduated high school early at only 16 years old and immediately enrolled into college. While taking care of a baby while still a baby herself and furthering her education Shan always found time to write.

The more she wrote and older she became the more passionate she became about her work. She then realized she had a natural born gift and that one day the world will enjoy her craft.

She is currently working on her fifth full novel Hated by Many; Loved by None set to be released in Novel 2012 with SBR Publications/TBRS and also her six release Tamar: A Rozalyn Novel set to be released in 2013.

At 27 years old Shan is working at achieving her goals one by one. She has dreams of doing stage plays and look forward to exploring that option in late 2013

She holds and Associates of Applied Science in Paralegal Studies, and currently works as a Client Benefit Specialist.

Shan is the single mother of 3 and will stop at nothing to see that they have a life that she only dreamt of.

Made in the USA
Middletown, DE
08 November 2016